Haunting Pasts

Trevor
Wiltzen

An Absolutely Enthralling Mystery

Haunting Pasts
An Absolutely Enthralling Mystery

TREVOR WILTZEN

Wiltzen
Publishing

Published by: Trevor Wiltzen Publishing
www.trevorwiltzen.com/contact

Cover Design: Trevor Wiltzen

ISBN: 9781777421243

Publisher's Cataloging-in-Publication

Names:	Wiltzen, Trevor, author.
Title:	Haunting pasts : an absolutely enthralling mystery / Trevor Wiltzen.
Description:	Edmonton, AB, Canada : Wiltzen Publishing, [2023] | Series: Mabel Davison mystery series.
Identifiers:	ISBN: 978-1-7774212-7-4 (Hardcover) | 978-1-7774212-4-3 (Book) | 978-1-7774212-5-0 (E-book)
Subjects:	LCSH: Women detectives--Northwest, Pacific--Fiction. | Missing persons--Investigation-- Fiction. | Serial murderers--Fiction. | Friendship--Fiction. | Detective and mystery stories. | Suspense fiction. | LCGFT: Detective and mystery fiction. | Historical fiction. | Thrillers (Fiction) | BISAC: FICTION / Mystery & Detective / Historical, | FICTION / Mystery & Detective / Women Sleuths. | FICTION / Mystery & Detective / Amateur Sleuth. | FICTION / Thrillers / Historical.

Classification: LCC: PR9199.4.W55753 H38 2023 | DDC: 813/.6--dc23

DEDICATED TO KERRY, ETHAN, EVAN, CLARA,
AND OUR FUR KIDS

FAN AND CRITIC PRAISE FOR THE MABEL DAVISON SERIES

"HOME RUN ... ABSORBING MYSTERY ... RECOMMENDED!" Phillip Zozzaro, US Review of Books

"5 STARS ... NAIL-BITING ... I COULD NOT PUT THE BOOK DOWN" Kim Zoby, Readers' Favorite

"A POWERFUL, INTENSE, whammy of a debut that was truly gripping and enjoyable to read." Andrea L., US

"What a FABULOUS DEBUT! I'm so thrilled this is the first in a series. Is this on your list? If not, it should be!" Susan Z, US

"A HAUNTING TALE ... EXCELLENT!" D. Donovan, Midwest Book Review

"I NEED THIS to be a series - a book series and a televised show! This book screams adaption!" Paulina M., Canada

"An ABSOLUTE GEM of a novel!" Renu K., UAE

"Mabel is SUCH A FIRECRACKER POWERFUL MAMA ON A MISSION." Haley C., US

"DESPERATELY NEEDED!" Scott Hayes, St. Albert Gazette

"There is depth and an ADDICTIVE plot that will keep the reader hooked." Matt Pechey, Pechey Ponderings

CHAPTER 1

Sunday, July 26, 1987

Mabel's day was a whirlwind. The last of the mine construction crews were about to leave Blue River with the first phase of the mine construction completed. Most wanted one last meal to celebrate and, naturally, Mabel's was the place to be. It was standing room only, every booth and chair filled. The workers sang rousing songs and encouraged Mabel, waitresses Sally and Molly, and the cook Kevin to take part in the music, dancing, shouting, and laughing. By the time the last worker left, her diner was down to six beers and a near-empty pantry.

Mabel's team kept up with the chaos as much as they could, but the dishes were piled high, everyone was exhausted, and Mabel didn't have the heart to make her staff stay for cleanup. So she let them off with a promise to return in the morning. Mabel then attended to the motel's front desk to check out the last of the departing crews. Their rooms, too, were left a mess. She had done her best to keep them clean throughout their stays and had trained the men to do the same, but they had worn their boots as they packed up, tracking mud from the day's rain all over her carpets. It was near ten at night when a bleary-eyed Mabel locked up. A busy week of cleaning awaited her, but she'd have time with the crews gone. And she was going to miss them.

Well, for the most part.

As a single mom of two young boys, guardian of her orphaned niece, and an accidental private detective on the side, things had become a little too much. The break would be bittersweet but welcome. Her guests had become friends and had stood by her when Karl Larson, the local drug kingpin, had threatened to burn her business down. But his gang had been stopped just in time, thanks to the unexpected help of her guests and two federal law enforcement agencies.

And Blue River hadn't been the same since.

While Mabel had nearly lost everything she had fighting for in this community, many did not see it that way. Larson's drug operation had supported a lot of local businesses, and although most wouldn't admit it, drug money was good money. And now that his demand for goods and services had dried up — with him in jail, his assets seized, and his men arrested or in hiding — finances were tight. To help compensate such losses, Mabel had increased her spending locally, which was welcome. But she wasn't. The whispers and glares behind her back had gotten a little too much, so she usually asked her staff to pick up supplies for her. But now that the mine construction was temporarily on hold, the bulk of her business would fall back to the usual motley crew of locals, truckers, and tourists, and she'd have even less need to buy from town, and those shops would suffer too.

Mabel sighed. Her feet and back hurt, it was late, and she needed a rest. As she hobbled out of the motel office, she frowned, seeing practically every light on in the upper story of her house. She'd have to remind the kids to save electricity with finances getting tighter. But at least, she'd have more time with her kids and—

She froze.

A man was lurking in the deep shadows of her porch.

"S-show yourself!" she cried out in fear.

He did.

And her knees buckled. With all the threats against her family making her anxious, this was the last man she expected to see.

Her husband — well, sort of ex.

Her fear quickly faded, but her anxiousness remained. "Bill, I'm exhausted," she said. "Why now?"

"Why not?"

Mabel stepped onto her porch. "I told you not to come unannounced, and it's hard on the boys."

3

"They don't know I'm here."

She paused. "Do we have to do this tonight?"

He handed her a bouquet of wildflowers — her favorites. "I'm here for you," he said, sounding as sincere as he looked.

She sniffed the scents while stretching her aching back and so Bill, like a gentleman, guided her to the rocking chair where he had been sitting. "Take a load off. You deserve it."

"Look Bill—"

"You must be exhausted," he said, taking off her shoes. "Here. Let me work that out for you."

"Oh Bill, I've been on them all day and—"

"Then best for me to ease some of the pain away," he said, rubbing her sore feet in the way she loved.

As she relaxed into the chair, she took a good look at him, noting his slicked hair and clean clothes.

"You look nice."

He hid his smile, still massaging her feet. "A shower and a shave never hurts."

She rolled her eyes at his self-confidence then melted deeper into the chair, counting the months since he was here.

"A hard-working woman like you needs to be taken care of."

She opened one eye, suspicious, but he wisely avoided her gaze, focusing on making her feel good, which might lead to no good.

She tested him by jerking her foot away, but he protested and pulled it back to work out her aches.

"You know I can't let them boys see you if you haven't changed," she scolded gently. "It's too hard on them."

"But I have," he said and leaned back to bring wrapped gifts into the light. "I got some things for them."

"They don't want presents, Bill. They want their dad."

"And that's why I got 'em these," he said, handing her a package. "Here. That's a baseball glove for Hector so we can play catch. And this one," he showed her. "That's a kite for Fred. We can use the school's ball diamond to fly it. And here," he gave her the last — a little box. And turned bashful. "I know you don't like getting gifts, but I got something for you too. A little thing," he added quickly, seeing her about to protest. "A treasure I found on the mountain, and it made me think of you."

She touched the wrapping cautiously. He had never bought gifts for the boys before, always leaving the birthday and Christmas shopping to her. It was nice to see him trying. Hector and Fred missed their father, though they didn't say it aloud as much now. While they certainly didn't miss the hard times, if Bill had really changed, it would be good for them all.

She opened the box and gasped.

"Oh, Bill," she said, holding up a tasteful green gemstone set in a silver necklace.

"Found that beauty up in the hills. It's as rare and fine as you are. And as soon as I saw it, I thought of you. I spent days tapping it out of that rock, it being so delicate like. And I used my fine tools, too, until it popped right up into my hand. Like this. Then with that last Amsterdam tradeshow I went to, I had my buddy — best man there is — work it into this silver. Here. See this detail?" He leaned in close to point something out, and she was almost overwhelmed by how good he smelled without cologne.

She touched his cheek tenderly.

His eyes shut to her touch, and he leaned into her hand, kneeling in front of her.

"Bill, you know I can't let you stay inside."

He nodded but said nothing.

She bit her lip and went on. "It's too hard on our boys."

He stayed silent and she didn't want that. She wanted him to start a fight so this could be easier. But he didn't fight. He was willing to take whatever she gave him.

She sighed, then pushed him back.

"Ohhh, I can't just send you off." But he said nothing, keeping his head bent. "Ugh! I guess I can give you one of the rooms of the motel. The crews all left today. And maybe, just *maybe*, I'll let you in to see them boys if you promise to be good and go to the motel room tonight."

He looked up finally and she expected his usual self-assured smile, but to her surprise, he was crying. Mabel pulled him in tight, deeply touched.

Angry shouts from Kerry inside at two laughing boys broke the intensity and they smiled at each other, breaking the sadness. Bill wiped his eyes with his big hands.

"What are your plans?" she asked.

"I got nothing," he said, clearing his throat. "Just as much time as you will give me."

She gave him a look that said *You certainly are saying all the right things.*

His cocky smile flashed before he turned serious again and said, "I've had a lot of time to think."

"Up in your mountains."

"Up in the mountains," Bill echoed. He breathed out slowly, and she could tell it was coming from a deep place. "A man gets lonely, for sure. But not just for his woman. For his family. I've missed a lot here, I'm sure." He glanced back at the house. "But I think about you and the boys every night. I even named some stars after you and I say my peace to you all before I put out the campfire and go to bed. It's a hard life up there and I don't know why I make it so hard on myself. I blame myself for that. A lot. I know I haven't been a good man."

She placed her hand on his cheek again, feeling closer to him than she had in years. Then she kissed him, his tear-stained cheek leaving a mark on hers.

Afraid she might lose her willpower and ask him to stay in the main house, she stood up briskly. "The boys will love to see you. Even only briefly."

He cleared his throat. Then smoothed his disheveled hair. "How do I look?"

She touched his granite-like features. "Like a mountain man coming home," she said, smiling to show no harm. "Very handsome." Then her tone turned a little scolding. "But don't you think all is forgiven. It takes more than a bit of sweet talk and a few gifts to forget the past."

"All I ask is a chance to prove myself, is all. Nothing more."

"I'll probably regret this."

He stood silent and contrite.

Mabel sighed, giving in. "Well, come on then. Welcome home."

He whooped, and she laughed. Then as he collected the gifts, she opened the door and announced, "Boys! I got a surprise for you! You too Kerry! We have a visitor."

The boys ran down the stairs, shouting and laughing, with Kerry trailing behind, then all three stopped short as Bill walked into the light of the front entryway. He slicked down his hair again, cleared his throat, and said, "Umm. Hi boys. I missed you." Then offered the presents. "I got some things for you all."

After a short pause, Fred broke the tension first, running into his father's arms. "Daddy!" Bill put down the boxes to pick up his son and toss him high into the air, both laughing. Then Bill looked to Hector and turned more serious as he saw his older son's pained face. He said, "Good to see ya, boy. I got something for you too."

Hector shifted cautiously, and Mabel watched closely, wondering what he would do. Then he ran to his dad and hugged him, and Bill hugged him back while staring at Mabel with tears in his eyes. Mabel's heart melted again seeing them embrace, and she couldn't help but cry. Kerry stepped over to her and the two hugged. Then Bill said, "Howdy, Kerry!" and Kerry beamed, caught up in the excitement of Bill being home.

As the boys pulled away, Hector was first to speak. "What gifts?"

"Well now," Bill said, handing them each a present. "Something for each of you to do with your old man."

They grabbed the gifts and ran into the den to tear off the wrapping paper, shouting with delight. Bill handed Kerry an envelope. "Got something for your college costs too. I had a gemstone hanging around camp that I kept tripping over, so I sold it, hoping this might help."

Kerry opened up the envelope and the whites of her eyes showed as she said, "Uncle Bill! You shouldn't have!"

Mabel leaned in and Kerry showed her the check. Mabel was impressed. "That's a kingly gift," she said.

"It's only money. Besides, that gemstone was getting in the way like I said and I was tired of it. It was too easy for me to sell it."

Kerry hugged Bill and he laughed and hugged her back. Then they made their way into the den as Hector and Fred excitedly showed off their presents.

Bill said to Hector, "We can play catch tomorrow." Then he turned to Fred, and said, "Same thing. If there's enough wind at the ball diamond, I'll teach you how to fly it."

"I've flown one!" Hector cut in.

"I know, and that's why you got a glove. A father and son should play baseball together and I heard you don't have one yet."

"I wanna play too," Fred said.

"Well then," Bill said, thinking it over. "How about this? I'll buy you a glove and get Hector a kite too, and then we can all play. Deal?"

Mabel watched them hug like no time had passed since his absence. She sighed, soaking in this moment.

Then Fred asked, in a tone that broke her heart, "Are you staying, dad?"

Before she could speak, Bill replied to Fred without even glancing at Mabel. "Well, I'm staying in the motel for now. And if she needs it, I'll be helping your mom fix things around here as long as she'll have me."

"Can he stay mom?" Fred asked.

"No need to ask your mother that," Bill cut in. "Now pass me that kite and let's put it together."

As they laid out the kite on the floor together, Mabel folded her arms and observed her husband, questioning whether this was the right thing to do.

But him saying all the right things made her hope, and so she put her fears aside and got down on the floor to be with her family.

Like it was Christmas.

CHAPTER 2

Tuesday, August 11, 1987

Mabel had closed the diner early so that she could use its kitchen to cook for a surprise party. Tuesday walk-in traffic had dropped to a standstill the past two weeks and if anyone did show up, she'd let them in anyways. Customers were treated like kin, and there'd be lots of food and drinks available.

She had organized a farewell for Kerry and Lisa, heading off to college — Kerry to the University of Washington in Seattle, Lisa to a beautician school in Tacoma. Mabel would deeply miss both. Graduation in Blue River was always a mix of emotions since most kids wanted to leave town as soon as possible, and she couldn't blame them. If it wasn't for the mine, there'd be little incentive to stay, not that working for a mining company was the be-all anyways. And with the local drug operation destroyed, a lot of money that had flowed into Blue River disappeared, and local businesses were firing more than hiring, leaving even fewer jobs for this year's graduates.

Fortunately, Kerry was over at Lisa's, whose mom, Consuela, was in on the surprise. At eight o'clock, Consuela would be driving Kerry home, Lisa in tow, but would make an excuse to pop over to the diner instead. From the kitchen, Mabel heard the diner slowly filling up. With the girls' school friends and their families, plus Mabel's staff, her friends, and Sheriff Dan, she was expecting over eighty guests. She had even invited all the Rotary Club members, a peace offering of sorts, given that they'd kicked her out of the club for her role in Larson's demise.

She wasn't yet ready to mingle, still needing to start the last of the dishes. Sally and Molly, dressed nicely, would help with the serving, and then join the party. They had been busy carrying the warming servers out to the counter for a buffet-style setting. Kevin had gone home early to clean up and would be back soon. Mabel hummed as she worked, reveling in the chance to cook in her diner kitchen.

Sally walked in and put her hand on Mabel's back to get her attention.

Mabel glanced at the wall clock and spoke first. "Getting there. I will start these last two pots and I got a few in the oven that should be ready in ten."

"Um, I think we're okay. I think we have enough."

Mabel laughed, busily stirring a soup, and said, "For eighty? We're barely over halfway there, luv."

"Um, I think we're good."

Mabel's voice broke a little. "What do you mean?"

"We have enough food."

The pit in Mabel's stomach twisted. She had been worried that the town's reaction to her role in Larson's arrest was still fresh and that some might not show. But not that many. Mabel's sadness welled up, and she covered it by stirring the soup a bit too vigorously. "So, not as many?"

"About forty, I think."

Mabel winced. "But with the girls coming and Kevin and others, we will be well past that."

Sally cleared her throat but said nothing.

Mabel bent down like she had to open the oven, but it was really just to cover her emotions. She said, without looking up, "I'll just finish up here and head out."

"I'm sorry, Mabel," Sally said and then left.

Mabel lifted her chin to stop tears from welling and expelled her breath in a whoosh. "Okay, Mabel," she said aloud. "Get over it."

She switched off the oven and the burners and put away the extra food she was about to serve. Even from here, glancing up and listening in, the party looked and sounded sparsely attended. Sally might even have been generous with her count, and Mabel had thought that was low. Mabel was done in the kitchen but carried on because she didn't have the heart to go out and see who hadn't shown. Only when the main diner lights were shut off to get ready for the surprise did Mabel wash her hands and prepare to join the party.

Molly rushed in. "The girls are driving in! Can I turn these lights off too?"

Mabel nodded, trying to seem excited, but as the lights in the kitchen dimmed, so did her smile. She wiped her hands dry, took off her apron, straightened her dress, and then put on the necklace Bill had given her before walking into the darkened main diner.

The energy was electric amongst the party guests hiding behind the booths, and Mabel edged down behind the counter. Bill came over in a crouch and kissed her on the cheek. "You look beautiful," he said, and she rubbed his back, more to soothe herself than him.

Consuela's car lights shut off, and the girls got out, laughing. Mabel smiled, always warmed by those two, loving them both. She glanced around to see who had come. Sheriff Dan waved at her, Kevin, Molly, and Sally were nearby, and the girls' closest friends were crouched behind the tables. Only a few parents were in the diner and none of Mabel's Rotary Club friends. Madeleine Proudfeather, the town's elder matriarch who got along famously with Kerry, wasn't there either. Mabel choked on that sadness. Bill patted her back like he was trying to help her clear a cough, but she waved him off.

Her invite had told everyone to park in the motel lot, expecting that all the trucks and cars would have given them away. But with so few people here, the girls might just be surprised. Consuela waved at the girls walking to the house to come back and then directed them to the diner. The girls changed direction and locked arms, chatting animatedly and seemingly oblivious to the guests inside. Then as the door chimed and Consuela, Lisa, and Kerry walked in, Molly flipped the lights on, and everyone jumped up to yell, "Surprise!"

CHAPTER 3

Sunday, August 16, 1987

A snoring Bill stirred, rolled over and put his arm around Mabel. Still sleepy, she purred and stretched, causing the motel's sheets to slip off her body. Having never slept with Bill in her motel before added to the thrill. She felt free and young again, the burden of ownership gone. And while she wasn't old at forty-two, she wasn't getting any younger either. She didn't expect them to end up here. But then Bill played with the kids earlier that day, and the boys were laughing and having a great time. Then Bill offered to fix some broken cabinets in the motel room's kitchenette, and with him wearing his white T-shirt and tight jeans, muscling in those cabinets was enough. It had been too long since the last time and three weeks since he had come home. When she finally made her move, Bill happily dropped his tools and carried her to bed.

She slowly eased out from under his arm to slip out of bed and put on some clothes.

Bill propped his head up to watch her dress. "You look good."

She shifted slightly to block his view of her well-earned tiger stripes from pregnancies but didn't cover up further. As a proud mom, she knew her body was different now, but the imperfections didn't bother her as much as they would have years ago. These days, she took pride in her appearance, but it was for herself, and not because she cared about impressing any man.

Mabel gave him a look. "Of course, you would say that."

"I believe it."

"You're foolish that way."

He smiled, putting his hands behind his head to look up at the ceiling. "Don't I know it."

She put on her shirt. "You did well with the kids today. They missed having you around."

"I missed them," Bill said, scratching his stomach idly. "Missed you too. Spending my nights alone on a mountain takes a toll on a man."

"Pfft? Mountains." Mabel rolled her eyes. "That's not the issue. You mean you weren't tempted once by those trade show girls with their tight bodies and string bikinis?"

Bill laughed. "Not one bit. When you got the best at home, why stray?"

"Well, that's good to hear. I'd kick you out again if you did that."

Bill chuckled and then leaned over to rub her leg. "And how about you? All those men pining after you…"

"Oh, please," she said swatting his hand away. Then she put on her pants, feeling the heat of his approving gaze.

Upon seeing his clothes piled up in a chair, she asked the question she'd been debating with herself these past three weeks. "Do you like staying here?"

"Hell, I'm used to sleeping on the ground in a tent. This is paradise."

"Compared to the house, I mean."

"Oh."

"I was thinking…" She paused to tamp down her anxiety, unsure if this was the right move. "You're practically in the house all the time, and it wouldn't be much of a change."

Bill sat up, serious. "You mean it?"

"It's not like all is forgiven," she said, throwing him a look. "And it doesn't mean you can stop trying either. But…" She breathed out. "You seem to have changed. And if you keep being good to the kids, I might not be so quick to kick you out again."

Bill whooped with glee before pulling her down on top of him. She laughed, feeling content and safe. But she still hit him on the chest nevertheless and said, "You brute." Then kissed him passionately. When she was done with him, she pushed herself away. "Now you've made a mess of my hair again."

"You look good that way."

She rolled her eyes and then got up to go to the bathroom to fix her hair and makeup.

But at the door, she paused. Then glanced back, pursed her lips, and flicked her hip seductively to let him know what he'd be missing when she wasn't around.

CHAPTER 4

Saturday, August 22, 1987

Humming along with the latest Whitney Houston hit on the radio, "I Want to Dance with Somebody," Mabel carried her cleaning bucket up to her home's second-floor office to finish the Saturday morning chores. Bill had moved in again and had already made a mess, his few personal possessions scattered everywhere. She'd forgotten what a whirlwind he was. She swept his dirty gemstone samples and field maps off to one side of the desk to set down the bucket. Then to her dismay found his over-sized geology map of Dead Man's Peak pinned on the opposite wall's corkboard. Originally, her photos and notes of the eight missing girls had covered it. But when six of the abused girls had been rescued during the DEA and FBI's raid on Larson's drug farm, she'd had removed those, leaving the last two on her wall. Now those too were gone.

"And here am I, forgetting about them, too," she said aloud. It pained her that their mothers had never stopped worrying, waiting, and hoping beyond hope that their daughters were still alive.

She scoured her office to see where Bill had put them. She grew more cross the longer it took until she spied a photo's edge sticking out from under his map. She peeled his map, popping pins, to find the two missing girls' photos underneath.

Their soulful eyes captured hers.

So young and similar in features, both had dyed hair, blue eyes, and a particular shape to their faces, they could almost be—

Could it be?

Mabel searched for her box of files next and found that Bill had used it as a bench to rest his tools on. She lugged the tools out of the way and then dug into her box to pull the file with the other six girls' photos. Then she tacked them back up on the wall to compare.

The other girls looked completely different in race, features, hair, or eye color. But the two girls still missing were the only ones that looked similar. It was uncanny.

She checked to see if they were related, and Sandra Hoffman and Tracy Richards, though of similar age, were born in separate counties to different parents. Yet, these two were the first of the eight to go missing and they were not found on the farm. As Tyrone, her DEA friend, had told her, extensive interviews of Larson's men captured in the raid turned up no recollection of them. The FBI's theories were that they were either killed soon after being abducted and buried somewhere in Blue River or else never taken there at all.

Both photos were police mug shots, Sandra for shoplifting, Tracy for intent to traffic. Both came from broken homes. But that was pretty much the extent of Mabel's insights into the girls, as she hadn't interviewed the parents yet. It was Lavi Arronson's legal assistant, Janice, who had, and maybe she hadn't asked the right questions—

Her attention snapped to a chilling scream outside.

She rushed to the window.

Her boys were screaming and being chased around the yard by Bill, pretending to be a monster. Her fear faded as she smiled, pleased to see him so engaged. He was already a big help fixing shingles on the roof and getting the motel back into shape, saving her costly repairs. With the mine's Phase 2 construction still months away, Mabel had a much-needed breather. And since Sally and Molly counted on their waitressing income, Mabel kept them on, giving her even more free time. And free time was not something she was used to.

Mabel touched the files holding transcripts of Janice's interviews with the missing girls' mothers. Neither mom would be able to look out their windows to see their children playing, as she could. It made her sad, if not outright depressed. Her work as an investigator was changing her, and not for the better. At times, she would start crying for no apparent reason, or she would catch herself angrily staring off into the distance, reliving the horrors of those two men who had tried to kill her at the mill or imagining the horrific trauma of those six girls rescued from Larson's farm. It embarrassed her when her customers caught her, and she would pass it off with a forced laugh. But if they only knew the pain and suffering of these girls.

Mabel chastised herself for forgetting them when no one else but their mothers were searching.

She toyed with the edges of the files, wondering what to do. She did not have the resources of a public defender's office — like Lavi Arronson, the lawyer who convinced her to get a private investigator license in the first place. She would have to do it on her own.

But where to start? The local police, state police, DEA and FBI had all looked at these cases, and people a lot smarter than her had found nothing. How could she compete with that? How many had looked at these case files and assumed that the girls had either run away to live in some far-off big city or were already dead from an accident, murder, or suicide?

Maybe that's true, Mabel thought. But these moms have no answers, and they would not forget. They would not lose hope for their children. She slapped the files onto the desk just as her sons' playful screams grabbed her attention again. This time, her gut twisted from guilt, and she winced.

Mabel opened Sandra's file and checked the family's address. The Hoffmans lived about an hour away, in Castle Rock. Not too far away from the wholesale grocery distributer she visited every Friday to pick up supplies for her diner. It wouldn't hurt if she paid the Hoffmans a visit on the way to let them know someone cared. Tracy's family was about twenty minutes further on, and maybe she'd have time to talk to both.

CHAPTER 5

Friday, September 4, 1987

Mabel drove Kevin's rickety van up to Castle Rock, a frontier town nestled in a broad valley and named for a nearby volcanic spire. Bill loved the area because of its geology, though she couldn't recall precisely why, and though most of his jargon went above her head, it was his enthusiasm she loved sharing more than anything else.

Like many Washington State towns, Castle Rock's main street was lined with storefronts straight out of Kenny Rogers' western, *The Gambler*. Beyond the main drag were the town's neighborhoods, some good, some bad. The Hoffmans, she noted, lived in the latter, where weedy, unkept lawns and dilapidated houses abounded. The look of a family's home didn't always correlate to how family members acted inside it, but

Mabel knew a run-down appearance didn't help the odds.

Mabel found the house quickly enough, but she was still anxious. Except for the wind rustling through fallen leaves, it was silent here. The front door's paint was peeling, the siding was a little worn, and the porch dirty. Not a welcoming home right now, or maybe never was.

Mabel cleared her throat before knocking. She waited politely, briefcase in hand, before knocking again. The scrape of a chair inside preceded soft steps.

The door cracked open, and a frowning woman greeted Mabel. "We don't take no solicitations."

"I'm not here for that, dear."

"Then what do you want?"

"I'm here about your daughter, Sandra."

The woman's frown softened a fraction. "She ain't here. I don't know where she is." Then she melted back into the hall shadows to shut the door.

Mabel stepped forward. "Please. I'm an investigator trying to find her."

"Police say she's a runaway. That she don't want to be found."

"Do you believe that?"

The woman stayed silent.

Mabel pulled out her private investigator license. She'd never used it before but thought it might help. "My name is Mabel, luv. I live out in Blue River. I just have a few questions."

Mrs. Hoffman took the card and studied it. Then she finally opened the door wider to let Mabel in, saying, "I don't mean to be impolite. But it's just me now, and I don't get along with my neighbors."

"Your husband's not home?" Mabel asked, glancing around the dusty den. "It might help if I can ask you both questions."

"He's not welcome here," Mrs. Hoffman said bitterly. "He left me with the bills. I work two jobs to make ends meet, and it's hard. I don't have no money, so if you're asking for some, don't expect to stay long."

"I own a little motel and diner myself, luv. In Blue River."

Mrs. Hoffman looked confused. "You own a diner? And a motel?"

Mabel nodded.

"And you're a PI?"

Mabel smiled and nodded again.

"Then you're probably not a good one working so many jobs."

Mabel laughed, not taking it to heart. Besides, a soft touch with an ornery person usually brought out the best in them. "I'm a single mom too," Mabel said brightly. "I do this on the side, but I've had some successes. Did you hear about the Karen Thompson murder, or the Karl Larson drug bust?"

Mrs. Hoffman took a moment to recollect. "Those two were in the news, sure. I ain't ignorant."

"I helped with those."

Mrs. Hoffman squinted like Mabel was pulling a fast one. "Didn't see your name in the press."

Mabel answered proudly, "It's not there 'cause I don't like the attention."

"Humph," Mrs. Hoffman replied. "Don't know about that. Those policemen were sure proud of what they did, putting themselves in all the pictures."

"Of course," Mabel replied, undaunted. "Most men like to take credit for the things women do."

Mrs. Hoffman smiled though she tried to hide it. "My name's Patricia. You can call me Patty. Please. Come in. I will make you tea."

"Tea would be lovely," Mabel replied with a nod. She followed her in and sat down at the kitchen table.

Patty was only in her fifties, but her kitchen was grandmotherly with tea cozies and little porcelain animals lined up on a windowsill facing the table, set for two. Mabel had seen only a few framed pictures in the den as she passed. All were of Sandra — Patty's missing daughter — and none included the ex-husband.

"Do you like herbal tea?"

"If you don't mind, that would be grand."

After placing the pot of water on the stove, Patty sat down. Her thinning gray hair and worn clothes made her look older. With an ex-husband and a lost child, this woman was hurting.

Patty looked at Mabel's PI license again before handing it back. "So what did you do on those cases? I heard a drug lord was jailed."

Mabel's thought went to Kerry's abduction, of her and Dan pulling Kerry, near death, out of that trailer of horrors, and then of Larson and his men showing up at her diner, intent on burning it down. Her emotions took over, and she couldn't speak.

Patty said, "It's clear you were in the thick of it."

Mabel swallowed. "It was touch and go, I tell you. My niece was abducted and almost killed."

Patty gasped. "You too? You had a lost child?"

"She's like the daughter I never had. She stayed with me after her parents, my sister, passed," Mabel said, not wanting to discuss her sister's cancer or her brother-in-law's suicide. "When she was abducted, it was the most horrible feeling in the world. But at least we got her back, she's been recovering, and now she's off to college. And my two boys are still with me. They're twelve and nine." Mabel paused. "As a mother, I know the wonder and pain of bringing a child into this world, but I can't say I know how difficult this is for you, with your Sandra still missing. But I will do what I can, I promise you that."

"Amen." Patty squeezed Mabel's hand. The kettle whistled, so she got up to pour two cups, then dropped the tea bags in and waited until it steeped.

Patty broke the silence first, settling back into her seat. "It's been four years now since Sandra's been gone. My husband, he, uh, couldn't handle it. So he left. Not sure which rock he crawled under, but he took his secretary with him, and she can have him, I tell you. Ten to one she's regretting it. Good riddance, I say."

Patty scowled as she took a sip, and then the pain sunk deeper into her eyes.

"Sandra was ... a handful, growing up. And I wasn't the best mother. I admit that. But I tried. She got into trouble with the law; did some petty shoplifting and the like, which shamed me. I didn't raise her to do that. Ended up hanging around with the wrong crowd, I guess." Patty sighed. "She did good in school, so I ... I didn't notice at first. I was just busy working and dealing with a deadbeat husband. But it's no excuse; I blame myself. It was a Tuesday when the principal came to my door. I remember the knock. He must have banged the door with his fist, and I was shocked to see him there. I thought Sandra got into some real trouble with the school this time. He tried to soft talk it, but I got him to lay it out quick. He said Sandra hadn't been to school for a few days."

She exhaled slowly, glancing down, and the pain spread across her face. "I told him we had been fighting and she'd stormed out to stay with her friend next door. He said she should still be going to school wherever she lived, and I agreed with him. I said I'd find her."

She shook her head. "I was furious, my daughter causing me such shame. Running away was bad enough, but she knew better than not to go to school. Good grades will get her out of this town, and I wanted her to leave, for her sake. So I went over to talk to her close friend, Kelly, next door. But Kelly said she hadn't heard from her for days. She even thought Sandra might be with an older man and was maybe staying with him. That was a shock, I can tell you. I asked if they were dating, but Kelly said no. It wasn't like that. Said Sandra was a little creeped out over this guy, but he had some sort of hold over her. She didn't know what."

"Now, I was truly frightened. I told this to the police; told them that Sandra was in trouble. They did nothing. They probably thought my daughter was typical town trash who'd hop into a car for drugs. But that's not Sandra." Patty's eyes turned fierce. "I know that doesn't make sense with what I just shared — but a mother knows. If Sandra doesn't like a man, she stands up for herself. And something tells me she was taken. But the police?" Patty spat out bitterly, and her voice rose as she went on. "I filled out a missing person's report. But that went nowhere. Then the detectives didn't show up for two days. Said they were busy. Busy? Can you believe it? A girl was taken. I was furious. I barely gave them the time of day and—"

"I read that," Mabel cut in but then stopped talking, somewhat embarrassed for reading the police files on the case provided by Lavi.

Patty stared back, confused until Mabel explained. "I had access to the police report. It said you were … belligerent. Sorry. That's what it said."

"That's being polite, I guess. I don't mind saying it. I was mad. The cops would show up here within an hour if it were some rich girl. But a poor kid? They assume she is off turning tricks for drugs or shacking up with some man and will come back later."

Her fingers intertwined and then twisted into knots. "My daughter and I didn't get along, but I birthed her, you know? I suffered for this girl, and I don't want to see her hurt somewhere or in pain or..." Tears came to her eyes, and Mabel's heart turned over.

Patty huffed as she got up to go to the sink, working herself into a visible rage. She picked up a dish with both hands like she was going to shatter it before she calmed and set it down gently. "You must think I'm a terrible mother."

Mabel got up to hug her, and Patty stiffened at first but then relaxed as Mabel said, "It's hard to be a mom. We all make mistakes. There are things I regret that I can't take back. I even hit my oldest son once, and that still pains me. Deeply. I can't take it back, though. None of us are perfect, and we all do things we don't mean in the heat of the moment. But at least, we can fix things when we break them."

"But I can't," Patty whispered. "She's gone."

The stinging truth of her words disarmed Mabel, and as Patty went back to the kitchen table, Mabel hesitated before sitting opposite.

Then Patty said quietly, "I'm glad you've come. I am. I don't think the police are doing anything about my daughter."

"I may have something that can help," Mabel said and then clicked open her briefcase — once Bill's — and pulled out the photos of Larson's men.

"Have you seen any of these men before?" she asked as she placed pictures of Larson, Kyle, and Eric flat on the table among Larson's other associates. Having taken these at a local skinhead rally months before, she didn't explain that she'd almost been assaulted that night and that the brute who pawed her chest still gave her nightmares.

Patty took out a pair of reading glasses and perched them on her nose. Taking her time to look at them, she finally pointed at Larson — the drug lord awaiting trial in a state prison. "I saw this man in the papers. But I don't know if that helps, any."

"Do you think your daughter's friend would recognize him? These men were part of a drug gang that abducted girls. This man here" — Mabel pointed at Kyle — "was the one who recruited them. And this man" — she pointed at Eric — "was Larson's second-in-command. He also tried to burn down my property and was one of the worst abusers of those dear girls."

Patty gaped at her. "He did?"

Mabel sat up straight, her gaze fierce, and she nodded.

"Well, I can ask Kelly if she recognizes any of these men. She won't talk to strangers, but she'll talk to me. She's a blessing, for sure, and in college now. She knows my daughter's in trouble and helps me when she can. I can call her now if you like?"

"That'd be amazing!" exclaimed Mabel.

Patty smiled, got up, and went to a corded phone in the den. Mabel only heard muffled talking sounds, so

Patty explained when she returned. "She'll be over quick. That's why I never minded when my Sandra would run off to her house, it wasn't far, and Kelly's a good kid."

Patty clasped her hands in her lap and stayed silent until the screen door opened and closed. Kelly walked in like she owned the place.

Kelly eyed Mabel suspiciously until Patty reached out to her, and both softened considerably beside each other. "Dear," Patty said to Kelly. "This is Mabel Davison. She's an investigator who does some other things on the side." Patty winked at Mabel. "She's here for Sandra, and we can trust her. She has some pictures she wants to show you."

Mabel arranged the photos on the table for Kelly to look at them. "Patty said you saw the man stalking Sandra. I was wondering if he's in one of these photos?"

Kelly leaned over tentatively but then, as she kept scanning, she picked them up one by one. Then finally, she shook her head. "He ain't here."

Mabel deflated. "Can you describe him then?"

Kelly nodded. She pointed to a photo of Pete, the man who had pulled a gun at Mabel's diner before a group of construction workers had walked in and scared him off. "It's not him. But the man you're looking for had that tattoo."

Mabel's eyes widened as she examined it, a white power tattoo that marked a Larson man. "He was in his forties, maybe. Wore sunglasses mostly, which was kind of strange since it was near dark when I saw him. He had, um, a thin mustache and kinda looked like a dad not keeping up on exercising, that sort, if you get my meaning. What else? Um, dark hair. Thin build. Wore a turtleneck, regular pants, and black shoes, I think. I've kept my eyes out for him since, but I kinda see him everywhere. He was just that plain-looking, you know?"

Mabel pointed at the photo. "Except for this tattoo."

"Yeah, that didn't fit. When I pointed it out, he tried to roll his sleeve down quickly like he didn't want it seen. Then he laughed it off, saying he got it with some buddies as a joke a while back. I thought it made him a creep, but Sandra didn't mind hanging around with him at first until it got weird."

"How?"

Kelly shrugged. "She just said he was a little off. But she didn't really want to talk about him much, said it was no big deal."

"Any other details?"

"Well, the brief time I saw his eyes they were brown, I remember that. But there was something strange about them. Like they were flat. I don't mean stupid, he sounded smart enough, and he sure smiled a lot but kinda in a fake way." Kelly paused to think about it some more.

"It's like … he was looking at you like you were some animal at a zoo. It gave me the shivers. Like his face was a mask, I guess. Yeah. Like he was hiding something deep down." Kelly stopped talking as Mabel absorbed what she said. Larson's eyes were like that, deep-set but flat and soulless. She looked back at her collection of photos.

"Are you sure it's none of these men?" Mabel asked, pointing particularly to Larson within a group of men.

Kelly shook her head.

Mabel frowned, at a loss of what to do next.

"Sorry I couldn't help more," Kelly said.

"Oh no, dear. This is helpful," Mabel replied. Then paused before speaking her thoughts out loud. "And just because he isn't in one of my photos doesn't mean he isn't hanging around with this gang somehow. Sandra has been gone for over four years now, and these photos are only a few months old."

"Four years, one month, and four days," Patty replied, as if from far off.

Kelly hugged her until Patty gave her back a thin, pained smile. Then they both stared at Mabel like they were waiting for answers.

Mabel didn't feel like she had any, so she asked Kelly, "Did you tell this to the detectives?"

Kelly grimaced, folding her arms, and took a moment to reply. "I didn't think they were paying too much attention to me, and they seemed to have their minds set already. But I can tell you this" — her fierce eyes widened in fear — "she hadn't left on her own. That man took her."

CHAPTER 6

Mabel honked before she backed the van to the diner's kitchen door. Kevin came out to unload, as most of today's weekly grocery run was for his recipes alone. He had recently started experimenting in the kitchen, and after a few trials, she had agreed to add his dishes to the rotation. While this meant the diner's menu was no longer entirely hers, Kevin brought a fresh change to the place — and the construction crews and truckers certainly enjoyed it.

Having raced back from the grocer to make her Friday catch-up call with Kerry, a scattered Mabel left Kevin to it. Settling into the motel office, she dialed the dorm's main number. A bright-voiced girl answered, and Mabel asked for Kerry and waited, looking forward to the call as a reprieve from the emotional roller coaster of the case. Since Kerry's dorm had only a single shared phone, these scheduled calls were a blessing, as Mabel could never get ahold of her outside this time. And although Kerry kept up with their first few calls, she was already hinting that once midterm exams started in a month or so, those calls might get bumped.

Mabel sighed.

She missed having Kerry around. Bill was great at picking up the slack, but he tracked dirt all over the place. It was bad enough Mabel had to clean up after messy construction workers as motel guests; now she had to do the same at home. While he often apologized, which was nice, how many apologies does a man need to give before it finally sunk into his head that it was important?

To give him credit, she thought, his nightly foot massages were to die for. Not to mention the nights when—

She giggled out loud.

A trucker walking to the bathrooms in the hall caught her beaming. He gestured to ask if she wanted him over, but she waved him off. She had no interest in men that way, other than Bill. Glancing into the diner, she approved how Sally had everything in order and was taking good care of the few customers remaining. Now if Kevin could only—

"Auntie! Are you still there?"

Mabel nearly dropped the phone. "Yes, luv. I'm still here. How's it going?"

"Fan-tastic!" Kerry laughed before she dove right in. "I'm so nuts taking six courses because the study load is gonna be a nightmare. But, oh my God, Auntie, is it fun. I'm learning lots."

"Teachers good?"

"Ah-mazing," Kerry replied, emphasizing each syllable and causing Mabel to smile. "I got one in particular — a Dr. Grace Bailey — teaching intro science. And get this. She's a geology professor who travels the world. Just like Uncle Bill! She almost got me interested in rocks." Kerry laughed again. "But you know, finance is my thing. Calculus is simple, duh, but English is going to be hard. Ughhh! I'm gonna hate that course. I have to read one book a week and it's going to be oh so-o-o boring. She's going to get us to read classics from the last two centuries. So, here's what I said on the first day of class, 'Just because a book is the first of its genre doesn't mean it's any good, right?'" Mabel shrugged but stayed quiet, unable to keep up. "But what else? Too many people in my intro classes — probably forty in each. Biggest classes on campus because they make you take them. Typical, right?"

Mabel smiled to herself as Kerry rushed on, thinking that girls never went to college in her day, as it was either typing, nursing, beauty school, or having babies. But Mabel hadn't followed any of those traditional paths either.

Having helped her family at the diner and motel since she was eight, she wanted something more. So, when her father had taken ill back in '62 and was planning on selling the diner and motel because, in his words, "Women don't run businesses," Mabel and her mother convinced him otherwise. While she had to drop out of grade twelve to do it, she took to it right away. Once in, she quickly learned that her dad didn't have much business sense either. But it was only after both parents had passed and the estate went to her that she discovered how indebted they were. For the first few years, Mabel did everything possible to pay off her mortgage interest alone and eke out a basic living. Then when Bill came into her life, he helped, of course, but it was only when the mine started construction did things truly turn around. But by then, she had made some gains. The 24/7 demands of a full motel and diner, week in and week out for months on end, paid off. At first, the mining traffic was only a trickle, but once the company executives knew they could rely on her, they held off construction of a second mess hall and set up a long-term contract for Mabel to house and feed the overflow crews. While hers wasn't a big place, the crews fought to stay at her motel and have their meals at her diner. The workers made good money, and they ate a lot. Though Mabel gave big tips to the staff, she did well on everything else. Soon, she was paying off big chunks of her bank loans, and her finances were finally becoming manageable, giving her some much-needed relief. While the bank would own her place for years to come, her time to own it outright was finally in sight.

Kerry then asked a question that pulled Mabel out of her reverie. "Sorry dear, what was that?"

"How is your case going?"

"Oh, I met the mom of one of the last two girls."

"Mrs. Hoffman? Or Mrs. Richards?"

Mabel was stunned. "How do you know their names?"

"I read all your notes remember?"

Mabel hesitated, not wanting to go too deeply into this again, because that was what had caused Kerry to attempt to infiltrate the Larson gang in the first place. But Kerry continued, her voice cracking. "And I ... I can't stop thinking about them. Knowing just a little what those other girls had gone through I—I ..."

Mabel cut in, "I wish you were never involved in that. I do. And I can only imagine the terrible things you went through. But I hope you're getting the support you need. I do really worry about you, all alone at college. I know you are making new friends, but you need someone you can talk to about this."

A muffled sob came over the line. "It's tough."

"Forget the case. Let's talk about you and—"

"No! Please. This is helpful. Tell me."

Mabel breathed out, debating whether to say more, but the pain and need in Kerry's voice won her over. "I think I found a lead, luv."

"You did!" Kerry shrieked, causing Mabel almost to drop the phone. "That's great news!" Then she whispered. "What is it?"

"Well…" Mabel paused, thrown by Kerry's roller coaster of emotions. "Sandra had a friend. A wonderful girl named Kelly, who I met too. She saw an older man with Sandra just before she disappeared."

Kerry's voice turned ice cold. "Was it Kyle?"

"No. And that's what's surprising. It was another man. Kelly gave me a description of him. Average height and build, brown eyes, a mustache. But get this, he had a white power tattoo just like Larson's men."

"Oh my God!"

"Yes, I showed Kelly my photos too. You know the ones I took at the rave and the ones you helped with. But she didn't recognize anyone."

"Maybe he left before he joined this lot?"

"Could be," Mabel replied.

"Well then, I guess…" Kerry paused like she was thinking it through. "You're just going to have to talk to Larson or his men to find out who this pig is." Mabel blinked, wondering how this girl could read her mind. "I didn't tell you this, but before Kyle drove me to the farm, he stopped his truck at the crossroads, and said something that surprised me. He tried to convince me not to go. Of course, like an idiot, I ignored him cause I wanted to check out that farm. But he seemed to have second thoughts about taking me there. Maybe it had gotten to him by then — what harm he was doing. I don't know. I can't explain it. The two pigs that held me — Pete and Ed — were just plain horrible. They looked down on Kyle 'cause Larson, it seemed, had some sort of pecking order as to who was allowed access to us." Kerry huffed in disgust, and so did Mabel. "Kyle wasn't on that list."

"Do you think he will talk to me then?"

"He might. Certainly, not those two who held me in that trailer. They hate women. But that Kyle ... I don't know. He was a charming guy. I can say that now when he wasn't so horrible. I could see why the other girls were taken in by him." Kerry paused. "That's why I didn't tell you. I thought maybe I'd be shown the farm first and they wouldn't try something right away ..." Kerry faded off. Then she laughed, surprising Mabel. "I can still picture you and Sheriff Dan barreling in. Him with his gun drawn even, wow!"

"Dan was the hero that night. I was just there to watch his back."

"No. You made Dan stand up for what is right. Though he's your friend, and I get it, but he also kinda let Larson take over the place by doing nothing. It was you who turned him around."

"I certainly used my mom voice on him." Mabel chuckled. "It also helped that the DEA was planning a raid that night and he knew Larson's downfall was imminent." But then she stopped herself, not wanting to take anything away from Dan that night, as they had been a hair's breadth away from disaster. "He does have a big heart, dear. And he cares about this community, in his own way. He was trying to protect us. There's lots of things he did behind the scenes we don't know about. He's just not good at enforcing the law."

Kerry scoffed. "That's his job, isn't it?"

"I know." Mabel sighed. "It sounds funny, saying it like that. But the law here isn't the law here if you catch my meaning. Blue River isn't free of extremists or criminal types with Larson gone. He didn't start from nothing, and this place still has its very bad parts. But it's getting better, thankfully. Dan, he's just one man. We all need to help him."

"Speaking of that," Kerry said. "Are you still getting blamed for running Larson out of town?"

Mabel winced. For most folks, it didn't matter that six abused girls had been freed, that violence was reduced in several counties, and that countless drugs were taken off the streets across the Pacific Northwest. It was the loss to their livelihoods that mattered.

"Folks are still hurting."

Kerry huffed. "You did everything for this town. I can't believe they treat you like this. You're the real hero."

Mabel struggled to respond, so she quickly moved on. "So, you think Kyle is my best option?"

"Oh, Auntie," Kerry chided. "Changing the subject again when you get a compliment. I can so read you. You know I tell all my new friends about you — about my kick-ass Auntie in Blue River who rescues missing girls. You're a rock star here."

Mabel blushed. "You helped a lot too, dear. And Dan did his part and don't forget the FBI and DEA raided those farms."

"It was you," Kerry affirmed confidently.

Mabel shut down, humbled. Then asked, weakly, "Can we change the subject now?"

Kerry laughed. "No problem. I've got to get going anyways. Studying, you know."

"I love you."

"I know." Kerry's voice broke from emotion. "And I don't say it often enough either, but I love you, too. I call you Auntie, but you're really like my mom now." Her voice dropped to a whisper. "I know mom would like that too." Then Kerry made a fast goodbye and hung up before Mabel could reply.

Mabel pressed the phone tighter to her ear, desperately wanting to keep their connection alive, but the droning dial tone forced her to hang up. She started to cry too. But her tears weren't of sadness, they were of longing, of remembering her sister and her husband who had passed, and of her pride, of her children growing up, of Bill returning, and of Kerry becoming the woman she was today. And while Kerry might be one less child to worry about being off to college, Mabel always would.

That's what moms do.

CHAPTER 7

Saturday, September 5, 1987

Mabel heard Lavi Arronson, the public defender who had recruited her for the past two cases, fumble the phone receiver before he came on the call. She asked, "How are you, luv?"

"Mabel! Nice to hear from you. We haven't talked in a while. How are the boys?"

Mabel shared the latest and then finished with, "I saw you on Dan Rather. That was pretty neat."

Lavi laughed.

Once a demoralized public defender, Lavi's passion for the law had been reinvigorated after Mabel helped him solve the murder of Karen Thompson, the poor runaway who'd come to a bad end at the hands of two killers in Blue River. The resolution of that case had given Lavi national press coverage. Being the second defense lawyer in the country to leverage DNA evidence in a trial, the State of Washington versus Winston Washington case, which cleared the young man of the charges, was cited as precedent in cases across the country. While Lavi wished Mabel would participate in the media interviews, Mabel consistently declined.

"I can't guarantee I can keep your name out of the press anymore. Dan Rather's on the hunt to find out who my mystery PI is."

Mabel grimaced. "Please do your best, dear." If her name got out, things would only get worse. Most of her old friends in the Rotary Club — or who she thought had been friends — were already avoiding her. "I've got enough worries with what I'm working on now."

"Oh!" Lavi sounded put out. "You're on a case again? Who recruited you?"

"Oh, it's not that, dear," Mabel said. "You know I'm not really a PI."

"That means you're still looking for your two missing girls, then," Lavi said, solemnly. "You know, the detectives think they're buried on a Larson farm somewhere and the FBI reassigned their agents elsewhere."

"That's a shame," Mabel retorted, "because their mothers won't stop looking."

Lavi went silent. His mother had inspired him to be a lawyer after his father had passed when he was young, and he talked to her most nights. But her dementia was worsening, and he started to reach out to Mabel more.

He finally cleared his throat. "Not many would keep up on this."

"I know."

"Well, then, what do you need?"

"I want to interview some of Larson's men."

"Who exactly?"

"Kyle. At first."

"That's easy. He's low level. Who do you really want?"

"Well, it's—" Mabel choked on the name, flashing back to the terrifying moment he was about to set her diner on fire.

"It must be Larson, isn't it?"

Mabel shut her eyes. "Yes."

"He'll be more difficult. He doesn't talk to anyone anymore who's not vetted by his lawyer. He's terrified about entrapment, I hear. But I know his defense team, and they owe me." He paused again like he needed time to think. "Okay. If you keep this confidential and write nothing down, I imagine I can set something up. I can't guarantee he'll talk though. He might just walk. But I can organize a sit-down for you."

She only nodded slowly as the shock was sinking in that she might face Larson again until she realized Lavi couldn't see her. Then she replied, flustered, "Of course, dear."

"Alright then. The records kept on his farms were surprisingly detailed and foolishly uncoded. He must have thought he'd never get caught. His defense team has pretty much written him off, but they won't tell him that. They're not cheap and he's already defaulted on a payment to them once. And if he does that again, they'll jump ship and his appeals will end."

"How soon can this be set up?" Mabel asked, a little dizzy from the excitement and fear.

"Kyle will be easy. We can visit him next week. But Larson may take a while. I'll need to talk to his lawyer, Jim Prescott. I'll take him to his favorite restaurant — Wong's. It's a nice, quiet place, away from the downtown hustle where everyone knows everyone."

"This means so much to me. Thank you."

"Anytime. But please be careful."

"Why? Because he's dangerous?"

"That, and …" Lavi sighed. "Just watch out what you wish for, alright?"

CHAPTER 8

Sunday, September 6, 1987

With the boys asleep upstairs, Mabel spent a quiet evening trying to teach herself to knit, but her lack of progress frustrated her. Having so much spare time was taking its toll. She was bored. Her feet were up on Bill's lap, and he was giving her a foot massage while watching *The ABC Sunday Night Movie.* When he was not fixing things around the motel, he was spending more time watching television than parenting the boys and that bothered her.

"Bill?"

He grunted.

"I want to talk to you."

He shrugged, staring at the television.

Mabel poked a toe into his stomach.

"What?"

"Pay attention."

"Movie's on." Bill waved at the set. "Can't it wait?"

She gave him a look.

"Okay, okay, I'll shut it off."

Mabel lifted her feet so Bill could get up and turn it off. Then she put her feet back on his lap when he sat back down. "I didn't say you should stop."

He laughed. "Is this going to lead to some cuddling tonight?"

"Dirty mind," she said with a look. But then he massaged a particularly sore part of her foot, and she got distracted and sighed. "Maybe."

Bill turned serious, as he said, "I see you put those pictures of the missing girls up again. Are you back investigating? I thought you were done with that."

"Those girls ain't found yet, Bill."

"Yeah, but you could have been murdered twice over with your past cases, let alone the motel and diner burned to the ground. Aren't you worried it might stir things up again?"

Mabel sighed and glanced towards the den window where their cozy reflections were framed by the forest's darkness. "I didn't know that would happen."

"And with what happened to Kerry? Jesus," Bill said, shaking his head, and Mabel felt a pang of guilt. "You're much too important to this family to put yourself in danger. Why not let Dan do it?"

"You serious?" she scoffed. "If I had, Winston would still be in prison and Larson'd be free, causing even more trouble."

"Well, a woman's not supposed to do things like that. You're needed here. For the kids. It's my job to protect our family."

"Let's talk about that then," Mabel said, moving the conversation to what she had wanted to talk about in the first place. "Let's talk about the boys. They need a father too, you know. They missed you."

"I know that. That's why I'm here."

"But you're not involved with them as much as when you first arrived."

"I'm busy."

"The renovations can wait."

"Hell, when I was growing up, I barely saw my dad."

"Your boys want to see more of you!"

"I'm right here!" Bill said, looking confused and vexed. "They can come and talk to me anytime."

"But they shouldn't have to ask you, you should ask them to join you. It's different."

"How so?" Bill asked. "That's not how it was with my dad. You did your chores and you didn't mess with him. If discipline was needed, my mom would do it. Because trust me, when we got my dad mad, I stayed good for weeks. That's how fathers and sons are. You do your thing and let the mothers raise the kids."

"You're not getting it. Parenting's not like that no more. It's different. Your boys have emotions, feelings," Mabel replied, taking her feet off his lap. "And it hurts them when you don't say 'I love you' to them. They say, 'I love you' to you, but you don't say it back!"

"What does it matter? Whenever I fix their toys, or fix the shingles on this house, I'm saying … you know … that," he sputtered. "By what I do for them."

"It's not about you getting it. It's about them. Don't you see?"

"Well—" Bill protested. "Did your father say I love you all the time?"

Mabel looked down. "I wanted him to say it. He just … never did."

"Right, cause that's what men do. We don't talk about this stuff. We show them by doing stuff. I don't understand why we're talking about this." Bill reached out to guide her feet back to his lap, but Mabel resisted.

He tried again, and while considering his opinion, she started to give in — until he asked, "We're still going to cuddle, right?"

She glared at him.

"What?"

She got up with a huff and left before she would say too much.

CHAPTER 9

Wednesday, September 9, 1987

Business had been slow at the diner this week, so she had given her shift to Sally. As a retired nurse and widower, Sally lived alone in town. But after that frightful night at the diner in the wake of Kerry's abduction, Sally had started saving for a singles cruise for seniors. Mabel was happy for her — though she couldn't imagine doing it herself. She was young when she met Bill and didn't want to ever date anyone else. An attractive man at sixty, he had a full head of gray hair, a deep tan, and a rock-hard body from tramping around the backcountry looking for gemstones or panning for gold. While his youthful looks got him lots of female attention at those geology trade shows, he had eyes only for her, and it touched her heart that he was so loyal. But he was a man's man. And that meant trouble.

She sighed.

"You meeting your husband?" a guard asked Mabel.

Mabel blinked rapidly, torn from her reverie — in line waiting for her appointment to see Kyle at the King County Jail in Seattle. "Oh no, luv. I'm an investigator. Besides, the boy I'm visiting is almost half my age."

"How can that be? We don't take juvies and I can't see you being older than twenty-nine."

She gave him a sly look. "Oh shush, you know I'm an older woman."

"That's fine with me."

The bell rang and the cell door opened as she added: "And I'm married too, luv."

He tsked but then let her through with a smile, so she touched his arm as she passed. She'd had worse compliments, but this fellow handled rejection well. And that's how she judged a man — how well he took a no.

She glanced around, reckoning this place was full of charming men who didn't take a no from a woman. But she wasn't naïve to think all abusers were in jail — she'd helped enough women around Blue River deal with abusive boyfriends or husbands. Though Mabel wouldn't call herself a feminist, she certainly believed in equal rights. Women's marches were happening around the country and if one ever came to a bigger town like

Tacoma, she'd go. It was time people stood up for what they believed in.

Another bell clanged and yet another guard waved her through the last gate and into a large room filled with a mix of well-dressed lawyers and upset wives with timid children in tow. Last time she had been in this room was to interview Winston, an innocent man, but Kyle was just plain guilty, and she had no sympathy for him.

A lone kid in prison orange sat at the table she was directed to, and his meekness surprised her. Kerry had described him as a jock, but what remained of him now was a twenty-two-year-old facing life in prison.

He politely stood up to shake hands as she sat down. "Nice to meet you, Ms. Davison," he said. "My lawyer said it had something to do about my case, is that correct?"

Mabel paused, unsure what his lawyer told him, but then dived right in. "I'm an investigator looking for two missing girls." Then she couldn't resist adding with a steely glare, "I'm also the aunt of a girl you had abducted."

"Oh, which one?"

"The last one."

"Gotcha." Kyle clicked his tongue and pointed his finger like he was shooting a gun. "I liked her. How's Kerry doing?"

"How do you expect."

"I bet she's in college now. She wanted to go to the University of Washington. I hope she got in."

Mabel nodded slightly, disturbed by his casualness about his crimes and not wanting to divulge any details about Kerry.

"Good for her. How is she liking it?"

"I'm not here to talk about my niece."

"Alright, alright. No worries. I'm just fucking bored in here." He looked around and then glanced back at her briefcase. He licked his lips and asked, "My, uh, lawyers said you'd drop off a care package. You know, in exchange for talking, I mean. Just leave it on the table and the guards will check it later." Mabel nodded and brought out the cigarette cartons from her bag.

"God, it's been killing me. Ran out last week." Then he rubbed his hands together. "I gotta talk about them girls now, right? Okay, bang away."

Mabel reached down to get a file from her briefcase, partly to give her time to hide her disgust. Then she pulled out the two girls' pictures and handed them to him.

"Damn. An FBI agent showed me those. You came a long way to waste your time."

"You barely looked at them."

Kyle flashed an irritated look before he lifted each one theatrically like he was examining it before he placed them back on the table and shook his head.

Mabel was at a loss. There was no lie in his eyes, but she didn't come here to give up so easily. "Well, if these girls weren't taken by you, who did?"

Kyle shrugged.

"Can you guess?"

He laughed. "I brought prettier ones into the coop that's for sure." The skinheads had imprisoned the abducted girls in an old, converted chicken coop in the forest behind a weed farm. "The boys and the boss wanted a few years older than these, into drugs, that sort of thing. Maybe it was the guy before me."

Mabel's brow twitched. "Which guy?"

"I don't know. I think it was a Tony or something." He leaned back. "Like I said, it was before me."

"I haven't heard that name before."

Kyle smiled. "Well, he started the whole thing."

"You mean Larson?"

Kyle laughed. "Larson might have loved the coop, but he sure didn't build it. Pete and Ed always raved about the guy who did. Some pencil-necked geek who brought the first girls in and shared 'em around. I guess he was the quiet sort, kinda kept to himself in the coop. But the guys didn't care if they got the girls, right? And by the time I'd showed up, he was long gone." He pushed the photos back to Mabel. "This wasn't work I'd aspired to, you know? It's just the stuff they gave me until I proved myself."

He picked at something between his teeth. "It wasn't all bad, I guess. I traveled around to recruit girls, go to parties, that sort of thing. But it got boring quick. And no one respected it. I was basically trapped doing this shitty job because I was good at it." He flicked off a bit of food from his nail. "I never understood why Larson wanted them. He could have got any sort of girl, right? Paid or otherwise, you know. Lots of girls were into it. And he did too, believe me. The guys shared their girlfriends around. It was expected. But why the coop, then?" He exhaled and shook his head. "Shit, I thought the whole thing was stupid. Someone was bound to look for them. And guess what, I heard these girls were the reason we got raided. Imagine that. Larson ruled this multi-million-dollar drug operation and it all goes down in flames because he kept a couple of strays. Funny, huh?"

Mabel couldn't hide her disgust, which he misread. "Yeah, well, I know. It's gone now. The boss kept detailed records too, like he was running some sort of corner store." Kyle glanced around to see if anyone was listening and then leaned in, lowering his voice. "What an idiot. Now I'm stuck here in jail too. I'm young, look at me. I don't want to be here. I'm facing serious time, for what? Trafficking runaways and because that dipshit Larson wrote everything down like a fucking businessman. Jeezus. The guy had names all over his files, keeping track of who got paid and for what and why. Guys in here are jumping over themselves to talk to the Feds. Some loyalty, huh? My lawyer says talk and make a deal, but I'm too low level to tell them anything useful."

"Can you describe this Tony fellow? Did he have a power tattoo, like this?" Mabel showed him a close-up of the tattoo Kelly had identified.

Kyle frowned. "Man, it doesn't help having that ink in here. Trust me. My crew is outnumbered five to one and are scattered in prisons across the state. I wish we were together in one, but there are only a few of us here and it's a fucking nightmare."

"Did he have this tattoo?"

"Lady, you listening? Like I said. If he was in our crew, he had the tattoo."

"Would he be in Larson's records somewhere?"

"Sure, why not? 'Cause, fuck, Larson even had our social security numbers and addresses and shit. Still blows my mind. Most of the guys here would kill him if they got to him." Then he glanced around before lowering his voice to a whisper. "I heard they have him in solitary in a state pen until his trial. Pretty hard to get to him, but the guys in here are patient. They got the time and Larson won't always be protected."

His pretty-boy eyes were all charm and his earlier meekness disappeared like he'd taken off a mask, but underneath was the same soullessness that she had seen in Don and Lee, the boys who'd murdered Karen Thompson, and in Larson himself. Her skin crawled as this clean-cut boy described how he had abducted girls, like he was reminiscing about his college football days.

She overcame her disgust to finish her questions. "Do you have Tony's last name?"

"Shit." He waved her off like he couldn't be bothered. "It started with a C or K or something. A kitch or catch, dis or dat. You got me?"

"Would Pete or Ed know?"

Kyle barked out a laugh. "Good luck talking to them if that's what you're thinking. They'd carve you up." Then he tsked before he smiled, but Mabel saw the devil behind his charm. "Lucky you're here with me, the next best thing to talking to Larson himself. Hell, I'll talk to you every week, if you keep bringing me cigs."

A buzzer rang.

The rest of the visitors started to leave and she automatically collected her photos.

"Hey! Do you think this'll help me get some time off my sentence?"

Mabel huffed, as she stood up.

Kyle frowned as he picked up the cigarette cartons. "Well, make sure you come back now. And tell Kerry I said hi. I'd love to see her again. See what she thinks of college life."

"Don't you dare talk about her."

Kyle thought about that before he grinned. "Well, I won't be in here forever."

"I said leave her alone!"

"She's sure a pretty thing, Ms. Davison. You bet I'll be thinking of her lots. She's the one who put me in here." Then he melted into the shuffling crowd of prisoners in orange jumpsuits before she could threaten him again.

CHAPTER 10

Thursday, September 10, 1987

M abel topped up the coffee mugs for Bill and Dan, who were sitting at the diner counter. Bill was telling a funny story of his younger days to a rapt Dan in his sheriff uniform about a misunderstanding between Bill's translator and the Peruvian locals that almost led to a regional uprising. Mabel only half-listened; she'd heard the story many times before and didn't like how Bill had nearly got himself killed. It reminded her of how tough his job was, living and working in remote regions around the world, and how it had shaped him. Though she valued his openness as a husband, seeing him be so hard on others, especially the boys, bothered her. She wanted her boys to grow up in a world that wasn't setting limits on them.

Dan burst out laughing so hard that he started to slip from his stool, so Bill slapped his back and kept his hand there, laughing with him until Dan steadied himself.

"God, Mabel," Dan said through tears. "Can you believe this guy?"

Mabel couldn't help but smile too. "That's why I married him."

Bill winked at Mabel before he squeezed Dan's shoulder. "I gotta go fix them rooms now. Nice talking with ya."

"Always," Dan said, catching his breath from laughing.

Bill went around the counter to kiss Mabel before he sneaked a cookie and winked at Dan. Mabel caught that, so she said, "Oh, go on! I expect that kitchenette in by the end of tonight, mister!"

"Yes, ma'am," Bill said contritely and then waggled his eyebrows up and down at Dan with a mischievous smile.

Mabel snapped her cloth at the departing Bill, who yelped, laughed, and went out the door. Then she wiped the counter where he'd been sitting. "Ugh, I'm always cleaning up after that man."

Dan took a sip of coffee and sighed. "God, that was good."

"The coffee or the story?"

"Both! But the coffee first, of course."

"That's right," Mabel said, and they both chuckled.

"That husband of yours sure has been on a lot of adventures. I bet movies could be made about what he's done."

Mabel looked out the diner window wistfully, watching Bill collect his tools on the porch in the fading afternoon light. "He's led a charmed life for sure. Of course, he married me. So that helps."

Dan lifted his cup in acknowledgment. "Here's to a smart man."

"Speaking of such," Mabel said. "Why wasn't Kennie at Kerry's farewell party?"

Dan choked on his coffee and then glanced around to see if anyone overheard. He leaned in and whispered. "Watch what you say about him."

She dropped her voice to a whisper as well. "I want to meet more of this man who captured your heart."

Dan recoiled again, glancing around. "Mabel! Would you ..." Then made a tapping hand motion for her to keep it down. "No one else knows about ... that."

"Well," Mabel said, putting a hand on her hip. "You shouldn't have to feel like you need to sneak around and such."

Dan gave her a stern look. Then motioned for her to come in close again. "You don't know what it's like. Hell, when Larson was around, I was terrified he was going to find out. He woulda done something terrible to me and Kennie, knowing how much he don't like them blacks and gays. But it ain't just him. I bet if more people knew I was ... well, with Kennie, there'd be trouble."

"You don't give people credit, Dan. Some would welcome it."

Dan gave her a hard, doubting look. "Like who?"

"Bill."

"Pfft. I bet!"

She put her hand on her hip. "Well, he's known for weeks, Dan, and it hasn't bothered him, has it?"

Dan's jaw dropped.

"That's right," she continued. "And do you know what he said when I told him?"

He slowly shook his head.

"He said, 'So what? Good for him.'"

Dan blinked. "Really?"

"He doesn't care about that stuff."

Dan leaned back, surprised. "But he's a—"

"Man's man, I know. Lord, how I know it. It irritates me sometimes I can tell you that. But trust me, all he wants is for you to be happy. We both do."

Dan looked out at the window towards the motel and said, "Huh. Well, I'll be." He sipped his coffee. "Mabel," he said, leaning in, wide-eyed. "If a man like Bill could be okay with it, then … I don't know. Maybe even my ma." Then he scrunched up his face and conceded, "But she sure don't say good things about the gays, I tell ya."

Mabel shrugged. "What if you told her the truth? She might change."

"Maybe," he repeated at last. She touched his arm to let him consider it and then walked around the diner topping up customers' half-empty cups.

By the time she'd returned, Dan had his Thursday paperwork spread out and was busy filling in forms. When she topped up his coffee too, she asked what had been bothering her since her visit to Kyle. "You think Larson would ever talk to me?"

Dan dropped his pen in shock. "That's a god-awful idea!"

"Let's say I might try visiting him soon."

"I think you should run away from that idea and him! Why would you ever do that? Oh!" He cocked his head back like the answer dawned on him. "Your runaways." When she nodded, he shook his head. "I think you need to leave things be."

She put her hand on her hip and gave him a stern look as her answer.

"I guess that ain't your way, is it?" She shook her head. "So, will he talk? I doubt it. He'll be pretty mad at you for what you done." Then he pursed his lips as he mulled it over some more before he added, "Can you talk to someone else?"

Mabel winced. "I did. And I kinda wished I hadn't. I talked to Kyle and he made a threat against Kerry."

"That's not good."

"I know. I was asking him about the two missing girls and he mentioned her. Said he'd be thinking of her in jail."

Dan grimaced. "Well, that boy should be in there a long time, I hope."

Mabel breathed out. "I hope so. But that Larson gang will long haunt us, I fear. Even in prison, they are causing trouble and making threats."

"Well, if you think Kyle was bad, Larson is a hundred times worse. Look. In them early years, when he was still small-time, I thought I could kinda contain him and such and maybe he would leave us alone. But he didn't, of course. I realize that now. And maybe if I had done more at the beginning before he got big, I coulda stopped it. But I didn't and then it got all too much too fast and I felt like I was all alone. Trapped even. Until you stepped up. Hell, remember that time with Winston at my jail? With those boys coming to bust me up and hurt that boy?" Mabel nodded, feeling a slight chill from that old scare. "Some of those local boys, like Ken, shoulda known better. But then there's the ones like Frank, as bad a seed you can find anywhere. It was Larson's doing, but they let it happen too."

"We all bear responsibility for that, Dan."

He nodded, taking a sip. "Speaking of needing to wise up, are those Rotary folks still upset with you?"

Mabel sighed and then bent her head. "Yes."

"If they only knew the terror of these men, just steps from their front doors, from their children, their homes. All the guns, the drugs, what they did. I don't think they would blame you no more."

Mabel stayed silent.

"It hurts being shunned for what you done, don't it?"

Mabel nodded, saddened.

Dan dropped his gaze too and added softly, "Or for who you are."

CHAPTER 11

Friday, September 11, 1987

Mabel walked into the Monroe prison and couldn't help but picture Larson's murderous gaze, haunting her since he tried to destroy all she loved that terrible night. That he had been caught in a motel — alone, hair dyed, growing a beard — and gave in without a fight did not ease her fear.

The guards led her into the solitary confinement unit, a closely guarded section of the prison, where she was carefully screened one more time before being left in a windowless waiting room. Unlike her previous visits to a jail, she would be alone with the prisoner except for a single guard watching from a distance. And though Larson would be shackled, Mabel's fear chilled her.

An older man in a dark blue suit, white shirt, and narrow tie, sat opposite Mabel. He wore a visitor badge like her. His suit wasn't flashy like a lawyers and his hair wasn't close cropped like the guards. He was studying some notes, occasionally glancing at Mabel. After a few minutes, he casually asked, "Who are you here for?"

Mabel had trouble speaking from the tightness in her chest. "K-karl Larson."

"The drug lord?" The man replied, sounding impressed. "You're with who then?"

"Just me, dear."

"No. I mean state, local, agency?"

"Oh, um, I'm an investigator."

"Private?"

She nodded.

"Defense or prosecution?"

"N-neither," she said. "Sorry, I'm just nervous."

The man raised his eyebrows and then nodded like he understood. "What's your angle?"

"Two missing girls," Mabel said, keeping her answer brief since her chest was so tight. "Abducted."

"Sounds interesting."

Mabel blinked, surprised, so he clarified, "Professionally, I mean. I'm here to interview a prisoner as well. A Mr. Ted Bundy temporally transferred out of Florida."

Mabel gawked. "Really? He's here?"

He reached over to shake her hand. "My name's John Ford. I'm with the bureau — more specifically, with the Behavioral Science Unit." He took out a card

71

and handed it to her. "I'd be interested to know what you get out of Larson. I heard he was involved in multiple murders, some he ordered, some he might have pulled the trigger on. These girls of yours, do you suspect he murdered them?"

"I'm not sure. At least, no one knows."

"You think he'll tell you?"

Mabel winced. "I don't know."

He examined her and she shifted in her chair, unsure what to do with her hands.

"Do you want a little advice?"

Mabel nodded.

"I see you came prepared. That's good. That's what I do. I do everything I can to prepare beforehand. But don't use your notes while you're in there. These men get paranoid. They don't like that. Keep good eye contact and if they try to control the conversation, let them, or make it seem like they are in control, or they'll clam up. Watch out for that. And if anything they say shocks you, whether they're trying to or not, act like it's normal. Trust me, they'll open up more."

Mabel took a moment to consider his words. "Thank you."

"Don't mention it. I imagine you haven't heard the term serial killer, yet?"

Mabel shook her head, embarrassed with her lack of knowledge.

"I'm not surprised. It's a new term we coined. It's when men — almost always men — murder multiple victims with significant time between each crime."

She glanced down at his card: Mr. John Ford, Behavioral Sciences Unit, Federal Bureau of Investigations, Quantico, Virginia. She looked up. "You came all the way from Virginia?"

He nodded. "I've done tens of interviews around the country. The subject I'm interviewing today is one of the worst. He kidnapped, raped, and murdered women across the country. I'm looking forward to it; he might add a key piece to our model."

Mabel hid her shock that he wanted to be here.

He nodded towards her briefcase. "Were your missing girls similar looking, that sort of thing?" She nodded. "Probably lost, runaways, doing drugs or turning tricks?"

She cleared her throat. "Maybe drugs. Um … living at home at the time but got into trouble."

He nodded. "If a serial killer did this, Larson or otherwise, check the papers, local records, that sort of thing. There's probably more than two victims. You'd be surprised what a little digging around can turn up. Ted Bundy here confessed to almost thirty. Can you believe it? And he's not even the worst." His fierce gaze rooted her to the back of her chair. "The female victims that survived called him handsome and charismatic but non-descript in a way. Very generic looking and—"

"—I have a potential suspect like that!"

He nodded, impressed. "Well, if you do find bodies — heaven forbid — the killer, if he's a serial, might go back to where they are buried. They do that for some reason. I'm still trying to figure out why. And oh, don't use the word killer or murderer. And don't blame them. You'll find out more that way."

A guard called out, "Mr. Ford! Step forward."

He replied to the guard, "That's me." Then he turned to Mabel and added, "Good luck with your interview."

The gate clanged open and he was gone.

Mabel sat back, stunned, then looked down and touched his name on the card. Here was a professional investigator, she thought. And though her anxiety returned, to her surprise, it had lessoned while talking to him. His suggestions swirled in her mind, and she threw out the plan she had prepared.

The buzzer rang, and she nearly jumped out of her chair.

"Ms. Davison!" The guard called out.

The gate opened.

She hesitated, dreading to go in.

"Proceed!"

Mabel closed her eyes and stepped in.

The gate clanged shut behind her, and the guard twisted the key in the lock before he directed her to a chair. She put her briefcase on the floor and sat down at the metal table.

A buzzer screeched and the opposite cell door cranked open.

She stopped breathing.

A slow scraping of shoes and a soft clanking of chains from the far hallway preceded Larson's appearance. And even in an orange prison jumpsuit, with hands and ankles shackled, his deep-set eyes in a pockmarked face terrified her.

The guard bent down and hooked the shackles of Larson's feet through the rings on the floor and the shackles on his wrists to the table.

The guard told Mabel, "You got half an hour."

Larson twisted in his chair like a trapped animal, and when he tried to scratch an itch and the shackles wouldn't let him, he violently rattled his chains at her.

She recoiled, horrified, as the guard shouted, "Watch it, Karl!"

Larson sneered like it was a game. Then his gray eyes bore into hers.

"I should've had my men kill you."

She gasped. Then tried but failed to dominate her fear as she replied, in an overly loud, shaky voice, "I t-talked to your men. They're mad at you."

Larson took his time to chew on that like it was bitter. "The records. Yes. I didn't think they'd ever find them. It must have been you. You told them."

Mabel didn't answer.

"Answer me!"

She flinched, clasping her hands tightly in her lap. "I had my s-sources."

"Your fucking sources," he repeated, disgusted. "My entire operation brought down by a fucking waitress." He spat to the side. "And a couple of stupid bitches."

His words lashed at her nerves, but her rising anger at how he treated the girls roiled inside her. Time slowed as she thought of Angela — Candy's daughter — repeatedly raped and abused, held for months in a cage meant for animals.

She looked at him, and this time was able to hold his wicked gaze with an intense effort. "W-why did you hurt them?"

He sneered. "Why do you think?"

"Why not just hire prostitutes? It makes no sense what you did."

He examined her for a time like he had misjudged her. Then shrugged without saying anything.

"Because of Tony?"

"How do you know about him?"

"Your men told me."

Larson's face contorted. He twisted in his seat again, but the chains wouldn't let him. "I'm stuck in here facing multiple life sentences. What can you do for me?"

"You are a scary man, Mr. Larson. You don't have to convince me of that. But I'm not interested in" — she was going to say crimes but remembered Mr. Ford's advice — "what you're charged with. I'm interested in what he did. The man who started it." She opened up her briefcase and pulled out the photos of Sandra Hoffman and Tracy Richards, placing them on the table. "Did he take these girls?"

"Can I keep these? I don't get Penthouse in here."

"Think of their mothers!"

"Mothers," Larson spit out, leaning back, his fire diminished. "I can't believe you brought me down."

She pressed him. "Do you know them?"

He didn't even look. "They're more Tony's type. He liked 'em younger, plainer. It was his whole fucking idea — the coop. Set the whole thing up and I never should have fucking agreed."

"Who is he?"

"Do your fucking homework!"

"Then tell me where he is. Please!"

He slowly shook his head like he couldn't believe he was answering her questions. Then he leaned in and whispered. "You want to know?"

She nodded.

He gestured for her to lean closer. "You *really* want to know?"

"I do."

"Then go fuck yourself!" He screamed, rattling his chains, shocking her backward and she nearly fell off her seat. "You bitch! You got me into this mess! You get me out! I'll tell you what you want to know if you give me less prison time. I'm tired of this shithole already and I'm going to be stuck here till I'm dead. You want to know about these girls? Fuck you. Get me out of here."

The guard shouted, "Enough Karl!"

"Those girls have mothers!"

Larson laughed derisively. "You think I care? They were playthings. Distractions. I could have had anyone I wanted and I did. I didn't fucking care who they were, where they were from. I could do it so I did it. But do you want to know who the real freak was? Your lovely

Tony. He loved to do some crazy shit to them. The guy was fucked up. Me? It was just part of the fun. But for him, oh boy, it was something else entirely."

"Are they still alive?"

"Get me some years off my time. Then I'll tell you."

"Please, tell me now."

Larson sneered. "You don't listen, do you? If you'd left things alone like those other fucking lambs in town, I wouldn't be here. You think I'm going to answer your questions? Fuck off!" Larson said to the guard. "Let me out of here. I'm done."

"Help me catch him! He's free, you're not!"

He scoffed. "Get me released, then I'll tell you."

The guard came by and unshackled him from the rings, and Larson got up immediately.

"Larson, please! The girls are running out of time!"

"I've got five consecutive life sentences hanging over my head. Do something about that."

Mabel looked down at the girls' photos, distraught that she had learned little of use other than confirming the first name that she'd already had. It made her ill.

No other leads.

No known whereabouts.

She looked up, but Larson was gone.

CHAPTER 12

Sunday, September 13, 1987

Mabel took her boys to the Castle Rock library, and while they ran off to the children's section, she combed through the state's regional phone books looking for the name of a Tony C or K. But the list of names quickly became overwhelming and was of no use.

She drove to Sheriff Dan's office in Blue River on the way home, kids in tow. This time, Dan didn't take much convincing to help. He'd let her use his computer in exchange for a free dinner at her home on Thursday. And while she was the better typist and could figure out the system faster than Dan, her search didn't yield any useable results either. The only Tony K or C in the system that seemed plausible enough was a Tony Ketch, and he'd died of apparent natural causes, though he was only in his late fifties, near Leavenworth in 1951.

Mabel leaned back and sighed.

"That sigh sounds like you're giving up. That ain't like you," Dan said.

Mabel gave him a look.

He raised his palms up. "I ain't the only law enforcement you know. Why not ask your DEA friends to check too? They've looked in all of Larson's records for the trials. I bet they owe you one."

Mabel blushed, surprised she hadn't considered that, and his smile broadened. She threw him another look. "For that, mister, I'll make you and Kennie a steak dinner. How about that?"

Dan blushed in turn and nodded but then quickly changed the subject. "I thought life would get easier with Larson gone, but these blasted machines are killing me. Why can't we stick with paper? This takes me twice as long!"

Mabel chuckled, leaving Dan to deal with it while she gathered her boys playing outside and took them home.

When she got in, Bill was nowhere to be found, and the kitchen full of dishes. She'd left a note for him to put the lasagna in the oven, but it was untouched. She set the kids in the den and then prepped the meal, irate. But it wasn't until having to wash his dirty bowls from lunch that she had enough.

When Bill sauntered in, rubbing his stomach, he tried to kiss her on the neck as she was serving the lasagna on plates, and she shifted out of reach. He pulled her in and tried to kiss her again, but she raised the spatula between them and said, "Where have you been?"

"Thinking of you," he said.

She gave him a stern look.

Bill released her with a sigh and went to get a glass of water. "At the motel."

"Did you see my note?"

He winced, as he leaned his back against the sink and gulped down the water.

"I can't do it all, you know?" she said.

He nodded, frowning. "I ain't asking you to."

"I am asking you for help. I left a note for you to put this in."

"I forgot."

"You forgot? How? You must have seen it when you left this place a mess. I clean up after my customers and clients. I don't need to do that at home too."

"What can I say? I'm sorry."

She fumed, not wanting to let his apology mollify her again this time. "I mean it, Bill. If you're part of this family, you help. The renovations are much appreciated, but I need your help at home too."

"Well, I—"

Fred walked in. "Are you guys fighting again?"

Mabel calmed herself for her son's sake. "Go on and wash up. And get your brother too."

Fred did as he was told.

Bill asked, "So? Are we?"

She sighed. "I don't want to be the bad guy here. But I need your help." He came over and put his hands around her hips, with a sly smile on his face. She frowned. "I don't mean that."

"You want me to help around the house."

She nodded.

He looked around. "You want me to cook?"

"I'm not that foolish. I mean to clean up the place. Do the laundry maybe."

He stood up straighter and saluted. "Aye aye, Captain. Where is it?"

"You mean you don't know where the laundry machine is?"

"Alright, alright," he conceded, chuckling. "Where is it? Upstairs?" She scowled, not impressed by his poking. "Okay. Downstairs I go."

"You're really going to help?"

"Sure, how hard can it be?"

"Alright then," Mabel replied hesitantly, not yet ready to believe it.

Bill stomped down the creaking stairs. Then as she heard him banging around downstairs, she finished setting the plates of steaming lasagna and arranged them around the table. As the boys ran in, fighting to get to their seats, Bill called up, "Um, Mabel? I need you."

Mabel rolled her eyes and said to Hector, "Go see what your father wants."

"Mabel!" Bill called out again, concerned.

Hector huffed, and then slowly shuffled to the basement door like it was the end of the world. Then his jaw dropped as he exclaimed with a laugh, "Wow! Jesus!"

"No swearing!" Mabel scolded him as she hurried to the top of the stairs to look down. "Jesus, Bill! What did you do?" She rushed downstairs to pull the plug on the machine as the washing machine foamed over, making a big mess. "What soap did you use?"

He handed her the right detergent but when she asked how much, he showed her the water jug she used to fill the iron.

"I stopped at your marking. It seemed a lot."

"Oh God, Bill, that's…. ugh!"

Hector came down and burst out laughing, as did Fred. Bill shrugged, grinning like what could he do. Mabel wasn't happy about it and her anger made them laugh the harder. At best, she ended with a thin smile, and then shooed them upstairs to eat dinner with a warning, "You're all cleaning this mess up after dinner."

The boys and Bill kept retelling what happened and laughing more each time. When dinner was over, she made them mop up the laundry area as she cleaned the kitchen.

Hearing them still laughing together downstairs finally settled her, and when she looked down at them doing another terrible job of cleaning, she softened. At least they were doing it together.

CHAPTER 13

Monday, September 14, 1987

In the morning, Mabel woke up early, went downstairs and stepped on one of Bill's discarded dirty socks. She could only shake her head. If her man could travel to remote, dangerous locations around the world to find rare gemstones, he could learn to work a washing machine. This expectation that women should be doing all the housework was overrated and besides, she had a business to run, let alone her investigations.

Looking forward to the change, she headed over to the diner singing her favorite Eurythmics hit under her breath, "Sweet dreams are made of this…"

About an hour into her shift, her good mood got even better. A trucker sat down at the counter and doffed his baseball cap as she filled his cup. "I took a wee detour so I could get some breakfast here."

"You've been here before, luv?"

"No ma'am. But my friend Charlie always says, 'You gotta go to Mabel's off I67 in Blue River for a meal. It's the best.'"

Mabel smiled brightly. "I know Charlie! How's he doing?"

"Doing a long run out to Florida, and he's probably talking about this place all the way there. Normally, I don't make no detours, but I've heard talk about Mabel's before…"

And as he talked on, she learned to her amazement that her diner was known at truck stops as far away as a person could drive in America. Apparently, a lot of truckers rated her place as one of the best pitstops in the U.S. While she'd known her reputation was good in the Pacific Northwest, hearing it had spread so wide was flattering.

When it was time for him to go, she fixed him up for the road with free coffee and pastries, and launched him on his way in a good mood. By then, most of the other morning regulars had left too, so she had time to call the DEA. The office secretary picked it up and asked her to wait as the director was coming out of a meeting. While she held the phone tight to her ear, she made a fresh batch of coffee — not wanting it to go stale in the pot.

As she made a quick dance move while pressing the brew tab button, Tyrone came on the line.

"Mabel! How are you?"

"Doing wonderful, luv. Except that my Bill's back in town and he's a handful, I can tell you that," she said, laughing.

"Bill is…?"

"My husband."

"Oh, I thought you were a…"

She chuckled. "Long story, dear. Bill's out of town most days — he's a geologist — and we had an issue a while ago and well, that's not why I'm calling. I got a favor to ask, dear. I got those two missing girls on my mind and maybe a lead."

"You mean with the Hoffman girl and, uh—"

"The Richards girl, yes."

"Why not call the FBI agents working that case?"

"They closed it. Or at least they ain't working on it. I guess they think those girls are gone and buried somewhere out on one of the farms."

"Hmmm, do you really think they're alive after all this time?"

Mabel shifted on her feet, her gut twisting. "I, uh, honestly don't know. I hope so but … I talked to Kyle — you remember him, right? He told me about a man who started the coop. And Larson confirmed it."

"Wait. What? You talked to Larson in person? How?"

"Just last week."

"Just last … What? I've been trying to interview him for ages! His lawyers keep shutting me out."

"Oh, I have a friend who knows a friend, that sort of thing, luv."

He laughed, impressed. "Can you get me in too?"

"I can ask, dear. But why I'm calling you is to ask if you still have all of Larson's financial records. I heard he kept personal information on all his crews so I'm hoping you can look up a name for me — a Tony C or K. I tried all the regional phone books, but it was too many to count. He would have been working for Larson maybe around '82 or '83 before he and Larson had a falling out."

A faint sound of scribbling came over the line, as he asked, "Is this an official case? Are you working with someone?"

"Just me."

The scribbling stopped. "Oh, that could be an issue. I can't share anything without an official case file..." He paused a beat. "But I wouldn't have cracked the Larson case without you, so do not — and I mean this — do *not* spread this around that I am helping you, alright?"

Mabel almost squealed as she danced in place, but she kept her voice cool. "Understood."

"And would you set me up with that friend of yours? I'd love to get Larson interviewed on record."

"I'll ask, luv."

Tyrone laughed. "Man, I am so glad you are on our side. If you get me in front of Larson, I'll owe you another one, let's just say that. Can I get this back to you tomorrow?"

"That'll work," she said, and they made their goodbyes.

Mabel pumped her fist and laughed, wanting to share the good news with someone.

Looking around, only Kevin and Sally were in the diner, but they wouldn't really understand why this was important. So when Bill walked past outside, looking so strong and handsome with his tool belt draped over his shoulder, a new plan came to her mind with a growing smile. If he actually learned how to wash clothes the right way, she might make this an extra special celebration later tonight — the kind that Bill would love.

CHAPTER 14

Tuesday to Wednesday, September 15-16, 1987

Phone for you!" Kevin called out from the diner kitchen, as Mabel finished her joke to a trucker with a laugh and a pat on his shoulder.

She scooted behind the counter and picked up the phone. "Mabel's Diner. You got the owner, luv."

A young man answered. "Oh, hi. I'm looking for a Ms. Davison — the investigator?"

"One and the same."

"Oh, um … okay. But you said—"

"I wear many hats, dear. Are you with Tyrone?"

"Oh, okay. You know him. I've got some information for you."

"To whom am I speaking, please?"

"What?"

"You didn't introduce yourself, dear."

"Oh, right. I'm Agent Franklin. I'm new."

That's obvious, she thought. "Okay, Agent Franklin, what did you find out?"

Mabel heard pages flipping on his side before he said, "We don't know who he is."

Mabel gave the receiver a look. "You could have started out with that, dear. I couldn't find him either, but Larson's records were meticulous I heard. How many men named Tony did he have on his crew?"

"That's what I thought because I did find a Tony Ketch," he said, brightly. "But I looked him up in the system and he died in 1951."

"That's not news to me. I was hoping you got some other numbers associated with the name — like a social security number, phone number or something."

"Nope. None of those."

"So, that's it?"

"Well, I think that person you're looking for is using the name as an alias and I got an address on him. It's an apartment complex in Tacoma." He rattled off the address and Mabel wrote it down in her notebook under the trucker's order for bacon and eggs. "I called the apartment complex as a follow up, but he doesn't live there anymore. Left in '82."

"Five years ago," Mabel said.

"Right … But hey, Tyrone didn't say much about what you're doing. Is this something to do with the Karl Larson case? I heard you got an interview with him. That's great. Which agency are you with?"

"Got to go. Order's coming up."

"Hey! I just want to—"

Mabel hung up while looking down at the address. She didn't want to waste this lead, however remote. Maybe an apartment manager or a neighbor might remember something, she thought. And with the diner busy today, she'd head over tomorrow on her day off.

She smiled as she rapped the counter with her knuckles.

* * *

Mabel's good mood carried over to the following morning when she made Bill and her boys a heaping breakfast. After her kids ran off to the school bus and Bill climbed the ladder to the roof to replace the worn shingles, she organized her briefcase with notes and photos.

When she left the house, she called up to Bill working on the roof, "Looking good, honey."

And he did too. The morning sun cresting the ridge was shining off his tight white T-shirt, though it was cold outside, and she could see her breath. He shouted down, "You coming straight home after your meeting?"

She nodded, shading her eyes. "If you keep this up, I might treat you again when I get home."

Bill's granite cheeks blushed, and he beamed as he made a motion to climb down the ladder, but she ran to the car, laughing. "No, you don't!" she called back. "You need to finish that roof first!"

He acted disappointed but blew her a kiss anyways.

Mabel turned on the radio and upped the volume to sing along with Whitney Houston: "I wanna feel the heat with somebody...," as it fit her mood perfectly. But after it finished, the radio announcer talked more than he played songs, so she turned it off and used the rest of the 90-minute drive to think about what lay ahead.

Tacoma, fronted by the ocean and framed by Mount Rainer, was another historic Pacific Northwest town that had fallen on hard times. The city's industrial downtown core was in as much disrepair as the apartment building and associated parking lot she pulled into. The complex's faded welcome sign displayed a collage of young families, and Mabel struggled to understand how a man involved in sex trafficking could have called this home. But at least it looked presentable enough in the morning light.

The address provided by the FBI included a unit number, #215. She walked by it and spied through open drapes, a young Hispanic couple living there, and Mabel wondered what the previous tenant — the man with the white power tattoos — would have thought of that.

Mabel stopped at the manager's office and knocked.

An older woman in her fifties wearing a baggy sweatshirt answered with a frown. "We're full up if you're looking."

"Oh, no dear. I'm a private investigator. My name is Mabel."

"Is this about the couple in 237? The police were there three weeks ago, and I don't know what they've been up to. I told those detectives that they're moving out at the end of month. And good riddance!"

"Oh, no, luv," Mabel said quickly. "It's about a former tenant of yours. A Tony Ketch? He was here at least five years ago."

"Don't know him. Why?"

"I'm looking for two missing girls. I believe he might know where they are."

"Missing girls? I don't know anything about that."

"I didn't catch your name?" Mabel asked.

"Crystal, and we run a good place."

"I own a motel and diner myself. Out in Blue River."

Crystal's frown deepened. "I thought you said you were an investigator."

Mabel laughed. "That's a story to tell someday. I'm also a mother with two kids, and frankly, I don't have much time for investigating. But the police aren't doing much about these girls and it's such a shame. Here, can you take a look at these?" Mabel opened her briefcase and pulled out two photos, having picked the ones their families had taken in happier times.

Crystal held both at arm's distance and squinted. "I need my bifocals for these."

"Do you mind if I come in then? Give you a chance to get a good look?"

Crystal hesitated. But her curiosity must have gotten the better of her as she opened the door wider. "I'm sorry. We don't get many investigators around here and when we do, it's never good. Come on in then. Do you want tea?"

"Love some," Mabel answered, brightly. Then she walked past a man with his feet up, watching TV in the den. "I don't know how it is for you running an apartment complex like this, but I struggle with all the repairs on my motel. It's never ending."

"Twenty-two years for this one and this's the original paint, or so I been told. We bought it five years back, and it's a handful, let me tell you that." Then she raised her voice to carry back into the den. "Doesn't help I got a dead-beat husband!"

The husband waved her off with a frown, still staring at the television. Then he noticed Mabel, brightened, and tried to pull his T-shirt over his exposed belly. He shouted at his wife while smiling at Mabel, "You didn't tell me we had company!"

Crystal ignored him, as did Mabel, and then Mabel said to her, "I'm worked off my feet, too. It was just me for a long time running my place. I'd kicked my husband out for drinking, but things are better, and he does a lot of the upkeep now."

"Wow, I wish I could kick mine out too," Crystal said loud enough for her husband to hear. Then she muttered, "Lazy enough."

"Bill's good, but we still have our moments."

Crystal looked off, wistful, sticking to her original point. "I think I would like that, kicking him out. Good riddance." Then she winked at Mabel and readied the tea.

After she poured the steeping tea in mismatched mugs, she got the ledger from her side office and plopped it hard onto the table before cracking its cover. "So you want to know where a former tenant of mine is. This Tony something." Crystal had her bifocals on but still lifted her chin to see better as she used her cigarette-stained finger to scan the columns. "Room 215, is it? About five years back, you say?"

Mabel nodded, eagerly leaning in.

"Hmm. Nope. No Tony. See? But I got a Samuel Ketch and a Janet Wray." She turned it around to show Mabel. "I can see that's not entirely good news to ya. Sorry. Not sure why he would've used this place as an address. Maybe this Tony character was a friend or relation of theirs?" Crystal closed the ledger. "I don't really remember that fellow either. He was only around for a few weeks when we bought this place and Janet broke up with him and moved out. A shame because she was a good tenant. But she didn't go far. She works at a bar down the street." She pointed out the kitchen window to a strip mall down the road. "You see it on the left side of the street there?" Mabel nodded. "It's a rough place, frequented by bikers and such. This neighborhood has only gotten worse since we bought the place, and that's a crying shame."

"Did this Samuel fill out any other tenant records?"

Crystal made a face like it was possible. "Let me check my other books."

When she passed her husband in the den, she slapped his leg to get him to sit properly. Then she came back and handed the lease form to Mabel in the kitchen. "Sorry. As you can see, I don't have anything on him. Just the girlfriend — Janet. She must have filled out the lease when they moved in."

Janet's occupation was listed as an office clerk for the Blue River Sawmill. That's interesting, Mabel thought. "Thanks luv. It's a start. Is this still her phone number?"

"Doubt it. Unless she paid to have it transferred, but like I said, she was running out of money fast. The mill had hit some hard times and a lot of people were laid off."

Mabel recalled that was just before Larson had secretly bought the mill to launder his cash, which made sense. Maybe Consuela, her friend who still worked there, would remember Janet.

Crystal went on. "She got the bartending job just afterwards. George and I go for a beer sometimes to watch the Tacoma Tigers. A piss-poor team, but what else we got?"

Mabel packed up her things, eager to talk to Janet. "Thanks again. I appreciate this."

Crystal made her goodbyes at the door and even her husband, still sitting on the recliner, shouted over his wife, "Come again!"

A ray of sunshine pierced the clouds, warming Mabel, as she stepped outside. And with the sun being a pleasant treat in these parts, she decided to walk to the Drifter's Lounge where Janet worked. But before she reached its beat-up bar door, a chill ocean breeze had swept in. Eager to escape its cold, she walked in and was promptly overwhelmed by a waft of beer and cigarette smell from the dimly lit interior. A few rough patrons eyed her casually as they guzzled their drinks or smoked. No one said anything until the female bartender, standing by one of the roughest, said, "Anywhere, hon."

Mabel chose the cleanest of the deeply worn booths in the back.

The bartender wiped her hands on a cloth as she made her way over. "The kitchen's closed till noon, but I can get you a drink. Are you waiting on someone?"

Mabel shook her head. "Is Janet here today?"

The bartender stiffened. "Do I know you?"

"Are you Janet then?" She nodded. "Do you have time to talk?"

"What's the problem? I said I would pay my heating bill. Or are you a lawyer I haven't met yet?"

"Oh, it's not like that. I'm here to ask about two missing girls. I'm an investigator, luv."

A look of concern swept over Janet's face, and she sat down immediately. "M-missing girls? Oh my gosh!"

Mabel took a moment, wondering how such a seemingly nice woman could be involved with a man abusing girls. "I have a few questions about a man you might know. Either one of your boyfriends, or maybe a friend of yours, who listed your old apartment as an address."

Janet sniffed, disgusted. "I've had a few doozies. Which one?"

"Tony Ketch."

Janet's jaw dropped. Then she laughed, "Sammie?" And she laughed again. "I think you got the wrong one. My last boyfriend was a biker — Ed. And that sommofabitch was a hard-drinking man who hit harder, believe me. If it was anyone, it was him."

"I'm sorry to hear about that but—"

"I can hit pretty hard too," she added proudly, or as much as her embarrassment allowed.

"Oh, I'm not talking about a Sammie. I'm asking about a Tony Ketch."

Janet smiled kindly. "He's one and the same. Only his mother and I called him that. See, Tony was his father's name, which he used for work reasons. I know, it sounds strange. But he was different. Because he and I..." she hesitated and then turned shy. "We thought we might settle down together. It didn't turn out, of course, but it seems like I have no luck with men."

"So, Tony Ketch ... is actually Samuel?"

She nodded, and Mabel started to realize why she couldn't find him on record. "Do you know if he worked for Karl Larson?"

Janet laughed. "You mean the drug lord? That Larson? I highly doubt it. Sammie worked in the same company with me at the time. That's how we met. He was a contract accountant for a sawmill and a few other places out near Blue River."

"An accountant?"

"Yeah. Spent a lot of time with management, that sort of thing. He was back and forth most days."

Mabel frowned and decided to press further, trying to explore every angle. "Um, did he have any distinguishing features, like a tattoo and such?"

Janet laughed again. "Yeah, one of the white power ones." She lifted her palms up. "I know that sounds strange too. But he said his boss got him to do it and he didn't mind because he thought it made him look tough — he had no idea what it meant. Really. He was no racist. At least, not when I went out with him..." She trailed off. "Well, he was getting into the harder stuff by then, so I don't know about now."

"What do you mean harder stuff?"

"Sammie was a bit different. He was a soft man, effeminate almost. I don't know how else to describe it. He was so gentle and kind to me when most of my boyfriends were total jerks." She looked up wistful. "He was so nervous asking me out, it was sweet. He said I reminded him of his mom, I guess. I don't know. I didn't quite see it." She touched her neck lightly. "He took care of me. Well, when sober, I mean. He got drunk once and was just mean — completely different. But he apologized and never drank around me again. And though he often worked late at the mill and he'd stink of booze, he was always sober by the time he came home. Told me management meetings were at a local strip club, and it was expected to drink." Janet shrugged like she didn't quite believe it.

"Was that Curt's strip club?"

Janet thought about it. Then nodded. "Yeah, that was the name." She laughed. "I'm sure he didn't mind looking at the girls on the poles too. But trust me, he was a lamb. Not the type of guy you seem to be looking for."

"Did he ever hurt you?"

"Um, only the time he was drunk, yeah. But after that, I laid down the law and he was good, like I said. He listened to me." Janet rubbed her arms. "I almost said yes to marrying him. I know he wanted it. But towards the end, I caught him with hard drugs in his car. At least, it was a syringe and drug kit. He tried to tell me it wasn't his, and he was only carrying it for a friend. But I didn't believe him and kicked him out. He begged me to take him back, cried even. That sort of thing. But I refused. I don't like my men into drugs. I have been there and done that and it's not my thing anymore."

"So, he didn't hurt you more than that one time?"

Janet shook her head.

Mabel frowned. "Did he have a thing for younger girls? Like teens, that age?"

"Do I look young to you?"

"Well, you look like you're in your twenties, thirties, luv, and—"

"That's kind."

Mabel breathed out. "I do mean girls about sixteen though."

"Underage girls? Serious? Sammie?" She thought about it but then shook her head. "I didn't see him stray or anything and I've lived a harder life than most. I think I would be able to spot that."

Mabel took out photos of the girls from her briefcase. "Have you seen these two anywhere? Was Samuel ever with these girls?"

Janet examined both photos closely before slowly shaking her head. Then asked, "Are they sisters?"

"Different families. Different towns. They were abducted though. Both aged sixteen and—" Mabel paused as a new thought came to her mind, comparing the picture to Janet. "You look like these girls."

Janet turned the pictures around and nodded. "I noticed that too. But I get that a lot — people think I look like someone they know. But, sorry. I just don't see it in Sammie. Like I said, he was a softy. He liked to comb my hair and paint my nails, and such. He did the same to his mom and was pretty harmless. You say he worked for Larson?"

"In Blue River. He wasn't an accountant though. A Larson associate I interviewed in jail told me he abducted and raped teen girls."

Janet's draw dropped. "Oh my God." She looked deeply disturbed and folded her arms as if she had turned ill. "Raped them? Jesus."

"Have you kept in touch with him?"

Janet shook her head and shivered. "I don't think I'd want to now. That's disgusting."

"He never mentioned anything about a farm? A place called a coop? Any of the fellows he worked with?"

"No," Janet said. "He didn't like to talk about it. Said it was boring work." Then Janet paled. "You think you know someone. But this is … ugh."

"Would you tell me if he contacted you?"

Janet nodded, staring at the photos of the girls.

Mabel reached out and touched Janet's arm to comfort her. Janet shivered again so Mabel got up and hugged her. Janet leaned into her. "Are you sure it is him?"

Mabel had to be honest, and she sighed before she said, "I'm still investigating. I can't say for certain. This is secondhand information so it's important I find him. If he is innocent, he needs to prove it."

Janet nodded. "If his mother's still alive, he won't be far."

"What do you mean?"

"Sammie's mother was in an old folks' home when I knew him. The old bat had Alzheimer's. He was a good son and adored her, but I thought she was just plain mean. The one time I visited her she put him down constantly and said I was a whore. I mean, what mother does that? He'd visit her at least twice a week, rain or shine. She was a poisonous bitch, but like I said, he was devoted. That's another reason why I can't see it. He was an angel to her."

"Do you remember the name of the home?"

"Englewood. Out by the highway. Her name is Angelica. Angelica Kerns. Her husband died when Sammie was six. He had pressed his mom for answers once, but she told him his dad died because he was a bad man — that God killed him. Like I said, nasty."

Mabel leaned back. "Does that place take visitors?"

"They did when I was with him, but I only went the once. She took one look at me and hated me right away. I often wondered if that was why he wanted to marry me — to spite her because she was so mean. I don't know. They had a strange relationship, and she gave me the creeps. But Sammie? No. I could almost guarantee you he wouldn't hurt a soul. He just wasn't the type. I just don't see it."

"Do you happen to have a photo of him?"

Janet breathed out, and then gave her an ironic look. "I burned them. I was hurt at the time, and well, I overreact." She shrugged like that explained it all.

Mabel was disappointed but thanked her and got ready to go.

Janet watched her put away the photos. "I know you can't trust anyone, but I'd really be surprised it's him. Do you think it's someone who is using his name or something? I'd hate for his name to be tarnished and it wasn't him, you know. Are you sure?"

Mabel didn't have an answer, at least one that satisfied Janet. As she drove home, she went over everything Janet had said and wondered now if this lead were a dead end. Up to now, she'd been sure that Tony — or this Samuel — was it.

But then again, the lead came from Larson and Kyle.

And they would say anything to get out of jail.

CHAPTER 15

Thursday, September 24, 1987

A week later, Mabel awoke at midnight to the
sound of her stairs creaking one step at a time.
Terrified, she grabbed the baseball bat from under her
bed before Bill surprised her by striding into the
bedroom when he was supposed to be at a trade show
in Cincinnati.

Mabel pressed her heaving chest. "Oh my gosh,
dear. Warn me, okay?"

Bill crawled into bed beside her. "Go to sleep," he
grumbled, and since it was late and she was exhausted,
she didn't press him, and only snuggled in closer. When
she woke up in the morning and was ready to talk, he
was already gone.

Once the kids were fed and on the bus, she searched
for him, eventually finding him in Room 107, where he

was adding a sink to a kitchenette. The mine crews loved the in-room cooking facilities, so she had decided to install them in all the lower-level rooms. She'd also be able to charge more when the construction crews came back, and that was a bonus too.

Bill was under the sink, cursing up a storm.

"Bill?"

He muttered a response.

"Why are you back so early?"

"Don't want to talk about it."

"I thought you loved that trade show."

"I did."

"What happened?"

He over-torqued his wrench with a clang, crushing his finger against the sink. He swore, punched his fist into the metal base in frustration, swore again, and then shimmied out from underneath.

She kneeled to look at his injured hand, but he hesitated to give it to her.

"Walter Hudson was there," he answered finally, and then glumly offered his hand for her to tend.

Oh dear, she thought. Walter Hudson was Bill's former business partner. Bill had discovered the vast mineral deposits under Dead Man's Peak in '79, which the current mining company now owned. At that time, he had brought in Walter as a partner and they purchased the land on credit in '82. But Walter soon edged Bill out — with the bank's help — and claimed the land for his own. Before Bill could stop him, Walter sold the land to CopperDex, which in turn sold its shares to another company. An announcement of the development of a mine soon followed. Bill took them all to court, where he faced a team of high-powered lawyers who buried him on technicalities.

Not only did he lose the case, but he also had to pay their outrageously high legal fees and, brief though the trial was, the legal costs cleaned him out. Mabel had to remortgage the motel and diner to cover the last of it. Bill's depression led to him drinking and then turned him mean and that's when Mabel kicked him out. He wandered around lost for a while, drinking at Curt's bar, a friend of theirs, but it was only when Curt suggested he go back to gemstone prospecting like he did in his younger days that Bill finally sobered up. Ever since then, Bill camped out on the peak, prospecting for weeks at a time, and had prospered again in his way. Though Mabel suspected some of his finds were on lands owned by the mine, Bill wouldn't tell, and she didn't press him because prospecting and then traveling to the various trade shows around the country selling gemstones at a premium made him happy again.

"Why was *he* there?" Mabel asked, now angry on Bill's behalf. She had never trusted Walter Hudson who had charmed Bill with his promises, and it had pained her to see her husband taken advantage of, especially considering how hard he had worked to find that deposit.

Bill rubbed his neck in frustration and said, "That son of a bitch is sponsoring the show with one of his new companies. Paid some ridiculous amount, like a hundred grand or more, for the title sponsorship. I didn't know that or I wouldn't have went! He even had the nerve to come to my booth." Bill shook his head. "As soon as I saw him, I couldn't think straight. I yelled ... maybe threatened him a little too." He smiled grimly before his anger returned. "Security came and separated us and the trade show committee chair — George, you know him — said I had to leave. That I couldn't be threatening the sponsors. He knows what Walter had done to me, but money talks, I guess."

Her heart turned over and she tried consoling him. "There'll always be another tradeshow."

He blew out his disappointment. Then looked at her, defeated. "Walter slapped a restraining order on me yesterday. His high-priced lawyers drummed that up quick. Five hundred feet, it says, which means any trade show that he goes to, I can't. The SOB was just waiting to do that."

She groaned inwardly. He loved his trade shows as they gave him a chance to make a living. Now Walter was trying to take even that, and no one seemed to see it but them. She put her hand on his knee, and he placed his large, calloused hand on top of hers. He looked at her and said, "I'm sorry."

"Oh Bill, you have nothing to be sorry for. That Walter is a true ... ugh!"

"You can say that again," he said, trying but failing to make a joke.

"I'm proud you didn't let this get to you like last time."

He sighed, looking away. "I wouldn't say that. I did go to a bar afterwards." He lifted his palms up at her gasp. "But don't worry — I didn't drink. I was tempted. It's hard, Mabel. Real hard."

She pulled him in closer. "It means a lot to me, you helping around the house, parenting the kids. We don't need that money."

He sighed. "I should get back to work here."

"Do you want me to stay?"

"No. Go on. I'll be fine."

"I don't want to leave you like this."

"Work is good for me. Like you said, he can't go to every trade show. I'll be fine." Then he picked up his tools and leaned backwards to face the bottom of the sink.

She wanted to hug him again but knew that wasn't what he needed now, so she touched his leg and got up. As she walked out, she glanced back. He had stopped working and covered his face with both hands. She desperately wanted to go back in to comfort him, but he preferred being alone. A proud man, he didn't like showing emotion. So, she shut the door and leaned her body against it, crying silently outside.

CHAPTER 16

Friday, September 25, 1987

Mabel pulled into the parking lot of the Englewood Retirement Facility. A long-term care facility where the one hundred or so residents had their own rooms, each with a narrow closet, a nightstand for photos and other trinkets, and a hospital-grade bed. The harried receptionist, busy on the phone, told Mabel the room number and waved her down the hall.

A man wearing a baseball cap pulled down low, a black turtleneck and tan pants came out of Angelica's room, and he passed her in the hallway. He was of average height with a thin build and a small potbelly. His brown eyes flashed as he walked by. Mabel turned and almost called out to him, wondering who he was, but he disappeared down the hall with a furtive glance.

Inside the room, a small frail woman in her early eighties was sitting in a chair, an afghan on her lap. Her wispy, white hair was neatly combed, her nails freshly painted, and she wore a bit of make-up too — black liner where her eyebrows would have been and bright pink lipstick. Her veined hands were shaking so bad, Mabel knew that if she had done it herself, she would have made a mess of it.

"Angelica Kerns? Do you mind if I come in?"

Angelica's stone-like face brightened, and she said, sounding stronger than she looked, "Come in, dear. Come in."

"Do you mind if I sit?"

Angelica beamed. "Please do. Are you my nurse for the day?"

"Oh no. I'm here to ask you some questions."

Angelica's cataract-clouded eyes searched for Mabel. "Questions?"

"Did your son do your nails? They are lovely."

Angelica's thin brows furrowed. "No one was in my room."

"I just saw someone leave."

"I don't get visitors at dinnertime. Have you brought my dinner?"

Mabel hesitated, realizing the extent of the old lady's dementia. "I'm sorry for bothering you this morning. I hoped to ask some questions about your son."

"It's morning?"

"Yes ma'am." Mabel noticed the family photos on her dresser. "Can I see a picture of your son?"

"Of course," Angelica smiled. She turned to the table and picked one up, which surprised Mabel as a moment ago she seemed completely blind. "Here he is. So sweet."

The picture was of a thin boy around six years of age, with a morose, much younger Angelica holding his hand. Decades younger in the photo, she was quite pretty. But the picture, like most of them, was grainy and out of focus. Mabel couldn't make out many details, but the blurry beach and mountain in the background looked very familiar.

Angelica touched the photograph. "That's a picture of our trip last week, so much fun!"

"Um, I mean do you have something more recent, dear?"

Angelica looked confused before she tilted her head at such a sharp angle Mabel feared Angelica had hurt her neck. "Recent? That's what you would like to see? No. Not many. I never liked taking pictures. He looks too much like his bastard father."

Mabel froze. Then asked, "Sorry?"

Angelica looked at the door. "Samuel! Is that you?"

Mabel craned her head back, but there was no one there. "Uh, no. It's me, Mabel. I'm asking about your son, Samuel, who also goes by Tony, and—"

"You're late!" Angelica shouted. "You can see I'm not put together! I want my hair done, you fuck! Look at my nails! They're terrible! The fucking s— who cleans my room has better nails than me. You think

111

your mother deserves this? You're a terrible son! Terrible!"

Mabel gawked, completely unnerved and a little frightened by the change. She sputtered, "Ms. Kerns? Your nails are done."

"Are they?" Angelica lifted her frail hands and stared so long that Mabel wondered if she had dozed off with her eyes open. Then Angelica put her hands down, her demeanor once again sweet. "Hello dear," she said, "Nice to meet you."

Mabel's skin crawled as Angelica went on, delicately adjusting the blanket on her lap. "The help here are lazy. At least the foreigners are. It's nice to see you. Are you a new nurse?"

Mabel shook her head slowly and wondered if she should leave.

Angelica touched the photograph. "I see you have a picture of my son at the beach. Were we talking about him? He's a very good boy, visits me often and does my hair and makeup. Do you like it?" Angelica proudly presented her profile to Mabel. My son does it for me. He loves me," she said, sweeping a stray hair off her head. "My son Samuel is a good boy, you see."

"I heard he goes by Tony, too. Do you know why?"

Angelica's thin voice shouted with rage, "He's still using that bastard name? His name is Samuel! I named him Samuel. He took that fucker's name in high school. He should go by Samuel, not Tony!"

Mabel palmed her racing heart while handing back the picture. "Um, I am clearly disturbing you, I'm sorry.

I'm going to leave now. But just before I go, do you mind if I ask where this photo was taken?"

"Bring it closer, dear. I need to look." Mabel handed the photo back to Angelica, who leaned over, almost to her lap to look at it. The top of her head was nearly bald and expertly combed over. Then Angelica lifted her head sharply, almost too quickly for her age, and came out of her trance. "That's near a dear mountain town we just love. We stay at a charming little motel nearby and spend weeks there. My little Sammie and I love the beach and go for walks in the forest along the lake for miles."

A chill ran up Mabel's spine. Could it be? she thought. "What was the name of the motel you stayed at?" Her father had named the place the Blue River Motel before Mabel had changed it to her own name to give it more of a homey touch after he passed. One of the few motels in the region, with its picturesque views of the valley, summer tourists would stop by simply to take pictures from the lot, especially those on their way to or from the state park nearby.

"Why at the Blue River Motel," Angelica said. "Where else?"

Mabel's eyes widened. "You must have met my parents. They owned the motel and diner at the time."

"Your parents?" Angelica said. "Who are you?"

"I'm Mabel. You were talking about your summer trips, that you took them in Blue River."

"Blue River?" Angelica said. "I'm in a retirement facility. What are you talking about dear?"

"That photo. In your lap. We were just talking about it. You mentioned you went for walks along the lake. I think I know that lake and beach. It has a little island on it. It's beautiful. When were you there?"

Angelica glanced at the photo, her head shaking, then she looked back at Mabel, suspiciously. "Why are you in my room? Did you come to steal from me?" Then she pointed a long finger at Mabel, and her voice grew louder until she was shouting. "Are you working with those s——? They steal from me. They take my money. Where is my purse?" Angelica slapped at her bed to find it. In a rage, she nearly fell out of her chair. Mabel reached out to steady her, but Angelica tore her hand away, and she was surprisingly strong. "Don't you dare touch me! Thief! Thief! Help! Help me!"

Mabel got up to go as Angelica kept screaming.

A female nurse in her fifties walked in, and as Angelica kept shouting, "Stop that thief!" The nurse took it in stride. "Don't worry ma'am. I see you haven't visited Angelica before. She gets this way. It's best just to step out for a moment."

Mabel did so, shakily.

When the nurse came back out, Mabel pleaded, "I'm so sorry. I didn't mean to disturb her."

The nurse calmly touched Mabel's arm. "Don't worry. She gets this way. Even to me, it's best we just let her rest now." Then the nurse guided Mabel down the hall.

"She's so—" Mabel stopped herself from saying vicious, not wanting to talk ill about her condition.

The nurse nodded. "I know. She can be quite a handful, to put it mildly. I'm the head nurse on this floor and I work almost exclusively with her as it can be hard on the younger nurses. Fortunately, her son comes twice a week to help."

"Tony?"

"He goes by Samuel here. But yes, Tony. He told me his mother doesn't like how he changed his name to his deceased father, poor dear."

"What's he like?"

"He's a good son. Maybe too good for her. Most of our residents don't get family visits. You see how hard this condition can be. But Samuel, or Tony as you know him, comes twice a week like clockwork. He dresses her, puts on her makeup and nail polish, and brushes her hair. He listens to her. He lets her rage at him as he does it, and it doesn't seem to bother him." She shook her head. "I don't know how he does it. He's like an angel because Angelica's mood swings are the worst I've ever seen."

CHAPTER 17

Sunday, September 27, 1987

With Sally on shift, Mabel spent the early afternoon back at the Tacoma library to read up on old news clippings as John Ford had advised. She bypassed the card catalogues and went straight to the microfiche section — transparent film storing printed information in miniaturized form — and found the reels for two local papers and the *Seattle Times* between 1977 to present.

On the monitor, the negatives were projected as pages that Mabel could magnify. It took an hour before she spotted an item of interest. She turned a knob to scroll through the immediate years before Tracy and Sandra were abducted in '82 and '83. But only one article in the *Tacoma Post* — just a few paragraphs deep in the local news section — mentioned the disappearances.

> A rash of runaway girls in the Tacoma region are leaving parents asking the community for help. Det. Janice Reardon, a police spokesman, said, "It's so devastating what drugs do to a community. Just look what it's doing to these families." Police are asking for any tips about these three missing girls and—

"Three girls?" Mabel stopped to whisper aloud.

She scrolled down the film to see a picture of Sandra, Tracy and a third girl, Karen Roberts, who the article said had disappeared while walking home from school in the Olympia region in 1981.

She replaced this film with another roll from an Olympia paper and scrolled through countless more articles until she found one about Karen Roberts. Now she had a new date of interest. Karen had left the local mall at closing to walk home on June 17, 1981, and her family had not heard from her since. The article did not say it had been an abduction, simply that if anyone had spotted this girl to call the police department. It referenced a spree of five runaway girls in the area, suggesting a minor epidemic of juvenile delinquency. There was another picture of Karen, this time a larger one. But the effects of the black and white negative projecting onto the yellowish blue screen produced a chilling effect.

But there was no doubt.

Karen looked like a sister of the missing girls.

Mabel's jaw dropped and she—

A reflection on the screen's edge shifted.

The hairs on Mabel's neck rose like she was being watched.

She whirled around.

The ten-foot tall book stacks hid most of the library, but the few people she could see, including the librarian, were occupied.

She waited a moment and then got up, scanning the spaces between the rows of books for someone hiding in between the stacks.

She stepped stealthily around the first stack and then slowly peeked into the aisle.

No one.

She stepped quickly to the second aisle, then the third. Each one, empty.

She paused, feeling a little foolish.

Then she rubbed her eyes, which were exhausted after scanning hundreds of images and multiple reels of microfiche. But clearly, with more girls unaccounted for, she wasn't done yet.

She went to the payphone in the hall to ask Bill to get dinner started, but she only got the answering machine. Next, she tried Kevin at the diner. He answered right away and, without knowing where Bill was either, offered to make a few specials for the kids and have Sally walk them over to the house. Mabel thanked him profusely.

Sitting back down at the microfiche reader, Mabel went further back in dates and found three more missing girls: early 1979, late 1981, and sometime between 1982 and 1984. These young teens had brown hair and blue eyes and were from poor neighborhoods — similar to Sandra and Tracy. While there was a substantial time gap between the first abductions, the gap was shortening. Then after 1984, she found two more missing girls that fit her profile, but no follow-up articles on whether any of the girls came home.

Now, ten girls had gone missing, not counting the six she had already rescued. But Samuel Ketch did not join Larson's crew until 1981, or so Kyle implied. But girls were going missing long before then.

Did this mean a whole new person or group of people were taking these other girls?

She leaned back, stunned.

The thought of more children facing abuse or worse made her ill. Her arms tightened over her stomach as the horrific stories of the six abused girls she had rescued flashed through her mind. Her arms squeezed tighter to stop the sounds, the rancid smells, the violations, but when it became too real, she bolted for the bathroom, slapped open a stall door, and threw up.

With the last of the echoing screams fading in her mind, she eased herself to the sink and rinsed her mouth.

Then she watched the water swirl down the drain for some time.

After another woman entered, Mabel turned off the tap, averting her gaze with some embarrassment, and hurried out.

Experiencing the aftereffects from throwing up, she eased herself over to her desk, and stood there awhile. But seeing now how late it was, she put her notes away and paid five cents per article to get printed copies of the stories about the ten missing girls and paid a little extra to get enlarged copies of the photos, which made their faces look like x-ray images. It wasn't great, but it was good enough.

She thanked the librarian and went out onto the street.

Thick tree trunks blocked the light of the streetlamps and cast deep shadows along the road and sidewalks. The wind had died, and the chill air transformed her breath into mist.

She clutched her coat tighter and started walking.

Soon, the crunching of snow behind her sounded like someone was trying to match her boot steps.

She glanced back.

A man with a baseball cap was following her.

Mabel started walking faster, the man matching her strides. He belted out, "Hey!" She ran the last few steps to her car, fumbling for her keys, listening to the boot steps approaching quickly.

Mabel turned, about to scream—

"You forgot this on the copier," he said, holding out a printout.

Mabel pressed her hand to her chest, breathless.

"You okay?"

"Thanks," she stammered, taking the sheet.

He looked at her strangely and seemed about to say something, but then simply nodded and walked away.

Mabel got inside her car quickly and locked the door.

She blasted the heat but couldn't get warm enough as she drove out of the city and then up the lonely, meandering highway toward Blue River. But each time a car's headlights flashed from behind out of the darkness, her eyes flitted to the rearview mirror and her nerves nearly failed her.

CHAPTER 18

Wednesday, September 30, 1987

P hone," Sally called out from behind the counter.

Mabel swept over and answered brightly, "Mabel's Diner and—"

Dan's voice cut her off. "I need you! It's an emergency."

"Oh my God! What's happened?"

"Computer troubles."

She glared at the receiver. "Ugh, start with that, will ya?"

Dan chuckled. "It's important. I got to file something this afternoon."

"Ask Kennie. He's better at that stuff."

"Not here. He's off on Staties business next two days. I need you."

Mabel was going to say no, but then realized she could use that computer, too. "Consider yourself lucky. I can be over soon."

"You got them cookies out of the oven yet?"

"You're pushing it, mister."

"Alright, I'm sorry," he said, chuckling. "Milk would be nice too."

"Ugh, you owe me. Remember that," Mabel said, then hung up.

Less than an hour later, carrying her care package of chocolate chip cookies and milk, she bustled into Dan's office, where he was watching television.

"Howdy," Dan said getting up to turn off the set. Then he lumbered over to the desk where his troublesome computer waited.

"Darn thing's acting up on me. Tried to fill out one of those I-300s for a traffic stop, but it keeps locking me out." He smiled. "Of course, I tried hitting it on the side a few times, but that didn't work."

Mabel laughed. "I know," she said, unwrapping the plate of cookies and pouring a glass of milk. "Some of my customers use those new fancy credit cards with those magnetic strips on the back, and they expect me to have some sort of specialized computer to read it." She shrugged. "I just do a carbon imprint like most people."

"It'll cause you twice the work, trust me. This one does, and they said it would be a time saver! What a joke," Dan grumbled, chewing on a cookie.

Mabel touched his arm. "Now what do you need me to do?"

As he explained it, she dove into the IBM PC 286 manual, figuring out how to use the floppy disc drives. "So fancy," she said. Eventually, she inserted the right disc, but it took them another hour to type in the information, Dan eating his cookies and grumbling all the while. When they hit print, the dot matrix printer screeched back and forth. When it finished, Dan carefully separated the papers along the perforations, but as he trimmed the paper's feeder edges, he ripped it almost in half. He swore.

"I can print another," Mabel tried placating him.

"Nah, I'll go get some tape," Dan said.

As he went to the supply cabinet, Mabel searched the police's computer manual on how to pull up missing person files. "Dan," she called over her shoulder. "Do you mind if I just figure out something here?"

He waved her off like he didn't care as he rummaged for the tape.

Mabel typed in the DOS command and pressed enter, holding her breath to see if it worked. A list of missing person cases popped one by one onto the green screen, and she covered her mouth from shrieking in delight. Then when it finished, she did a little dance in her seat and hit print. The printer screeched again, and Dan covered his ears and grumbled, "Damn, that sound's going to drive me crazy. What's it doing now?"

"Printing missing person cases."

"Eh? I'm not doing any—" He stopped and eyed Mabel sternly. "You got half the community mad at you for putting Larson in prison. Do you want the other half mad too? Sheesh."

"Oh, stop, luv. I got this covered. This is still the same case."

"The Tony one?"

She nodded. "That's his father's name. His real name is Samuel, which is why I missed him the first time."

"He took on an alias? Hmmm. Shady." Then his brow creased as he thought some more about it. "But I don't remember no Samuel either. While I never met every guy on Larson's crews, heck, I'm surprised I didn't bump into this one if he was so important."

"Consuela doesn't remember him either." Consuela, who worked in the mill's office, had more than once risked her job to seek out information to help Mabel with her cases. That the mill was still operating was a bit of a miracle since Larson had used it as a money-laundering operation. But with him gone, three crew shifts a day went down to one, and Mabel doubted it would last. "She can't check his personnel file either since most of those are still with the DEA. And she doesn't expect them back soon."

"Dead end then?"

"No," Mabel said, sounding defensive. "I've already met with Samuel's mother. She has the Alzheimer's.

While I haven't met the son yet, I hope to soon since he visits his mother often."

"But why check missing person files? I thought you knew who was missing. How many more do you think?"

"Ten."

Dan's jaw dropped.

"Maybe more," she added, picking up the pages from the printer and scanning the information. Right away, she recognized several names, but when the list continued onto the second page, her gut twisted and she put her hand to her mouth. "Oh my God," she said, handing the sheets to Dan.

Dan flipped between the pages, and his mouth slowly dropped open too, until he exclaimed, "There's forty-seven on this list! Do you think they're all related to your perp?"

"I don't know. I found ten of these scanning newspapers in the library — but not this many."

He handed back the list. "You know, some of 'em really could be runaways. Maybe came to natural ends too. There just can't be forty-seven different killers out there, killing people for the hell of it. It don't make no sense."

"Maybe there's just one."

"Killing forty-seven?" Dan scoffed. "The guy would need to be killing people left, right and center. He would've been caught by now. Look at Larson."

"After how many years though?"

Dan made a face like he got her point. "But still," he said, handing it back.

Mabel quickly scanned the girls' ages listed and said, "Maybe it's not all of these. But the ten I read about are remarkably similar cases — same looks, age, backgrounds, that sort of thing. And that scares me."

Dan hitched up his pants, sitting in the chair opposite. "Consider this, okay? Maybe they're all just runaways. I mean it. You know how it is here. Lots of kids run from homes that ain't so good. A few families right here in Blue River have had kids disappear. I know they ain't dead or taken because they come back after a few years, with some good stories to tell, let me tell ya. You remember Lester Crawchuck? Left at sixteen, back at nineteen. Made a fortune on those fishing boats up in Alaska and now he works at the mill and never leaves town. Married with a good family too."

"These are young girls, not boys."

Dan scrunched his face like she scored another point. "True. But I can't see someone killing fifty girls, let alone ten. I think you're on a wild goose chase here."

Mabel looked down at the printout, her finger tracing the list of names. "Maybe so. I hope so. But I don't see anyone else looking for them. These girls need someone at least to ask questions."

Dan relented, grabbed another cookie, and took a bite. Pointing the half-eaten cookie at the list, he said "Don't tell anyone I let you have that."

She nodded as she got up. "You coming by Thursday for paperwork and pie?"

"Always," he said, and they touched hands before she made her goodbye.

Back at her house, Mabel parked the car in the gravel drive but didn't get out. With the boys being watched by a sitter inside, if she went in, she'd be swarmed and wouldn't have time to look at this list till evening.

She spread out the printout and began reading. While all the women and girls lived in the northwest, only seventeen were in their mid-teens and fit her profile. But the printout didn't go into too many details about their cases. That meant heading back to the Tacoma library again. While she was not eager to scan through microfiche reels again, maybe the librarian had one of those fancy computers like Dan's that could make it easier.

Packing up her stuff, she noticed the door open on Room 108 and, figuring it was Bill, headed over to talk. The door was open, the lights on, and his tools were on the half-finished kitchenette, but he wasn't here. About to leave, she spied an empty beer can in the corner.

That's odd, she thought.

She'd cleaned all these rooms once the construction workers had left. Hundreds of empties had been left and a few still unopened, but it was possible she missed a couple. She walked over and picked up the can. It didn't feel cold, which was a good sign. But when she shook it, a small amount of liquid sloshed inside.

She frowned.

Ever since that Walter Hudson had got Bill banned from the Cincinnati trade show, Mabel's biggest fear was that Bill would turn to drink again.

For the boys' sake, she couldn't allow that.

She stood there a moment, frozen by worry. Then she tossed the can in the large industrial trash filled with construction waste and went looking for him.

Bill was walking out of the house, and when he spotted her, he smiled brightly and rushed over to give her a kiss. She let him, more to see if she could smell beer off him than anything else. "Are you okay?"

"I'm fine," he replied.

"You'd tell me if there is a problem, right?"

"Sure."

"You promise?"

"What's wrong?"

"I mean if you're drinking again, right?"

His smile fell as his face turned to stone. "Of course."

Mabel examined him closely. But as good as she was reading strangers, she couldn't read her husband — it was what both excited and frustrated her about him.

But instead of grilling him, to her surprise, she gave him a long, deep hug, and when he started lightly stroking the back of her hair, she closed her eyes, inhaled his manly scent, and prayed.

CHAPTER 19

Saturday, October 3, 1987

When Mabel got home after a long afternoon at the Tacoma library, the sound of the boys' laughter and the aroma of a roast lured her to the kitchen. The boys were cutting up the bread and setting the table while an apron-clad Bill made a mess of draining boiled vegetables into a strainer.

"Mom!" Fred and Hector dropped what they were doing and rushed to hug her.

"Guess what we're doing?" Fred asked.

"I can see it," Mabel said, smiling through her disbelief.

Bill came over and gave her a kiss and her toes twitched, surprised he was actually cooking. "What's this?" She asked. He shrugged nonchalantly, but she could tell he was playing it up. "I'm impressed," she added. "It smells good."

"Look at this, Mom," Hector said, grabbing her hand and showing her the slices of bread.

"Very impressive."

"And this too, Mom!" Fred cut in. "I set the plates."

"Wonderful, dears."

The oven door creaked, and she turned to see Bill pull out a steaming roast with a flourish. Right away she noticed he had forgotten the thyme, but it smelled good nonetheless. He fussed with placing the roast on the counter and she went to help, but he set it aside on the rack and playfully slapped her hand away. "I got it. You wash up. It should be ready when you come back."

Mabel gave him a hug, but his hands were full, so she secretly squeezed his bum, making him smile even wider. "You keep this up," she said. "There might be dessert for you later tonight."

"We got dessert, Mommie! It's ice cream!" Fred shouted, misunderstanding her.

"That's great, dear," Mabel said to her son, giving him a hug too.

After she went upstairs to wash up, the boys seated her at the head of the table. She got the shivers feeling so special.

"Smells wonderful."

Fred placed a napkin on her lap and then handed her the potatoes. Hector then handed her the vegetables. With no chance to serve herself, Bill stepped in. "She only has two hands, boys. Give her time."

While the roast was dry and the vegetables were undercooked, Mabel savored every bite. When they finished eating, the boys ran off to play and Bill kissed her as he walked out. "Got to finish room 108."

She happily set down her napkin, a proud mom and wife.

Then she glanced around.

Her smile fell at the mess of dishes.

Bill had dirtied almost every pot in the house, and it was nearly forty-five minutes before Mabel had everything cleaned up. But she got it done. Then she gave herself permission to take time for herself. Wiping her hands dry, she picked up her briefcase from the foyer and marched past the kids playing in the den and up to her second-floor office. Bill's maps and tools had found their way back to the desk so she banished them to the closet again so she could lay out her files and photos to tack to the wallboard.

The first thing she pinned was the printout from the library. Thankfully, the librarian's computer search had saved Mabel a lot of time. Next, she sorted the photocopied press articles on all forty-seven missing persons and the thirty-odd associated photos. Out of these, she tacked up photos for fifteen of the seventeen missing teens. Twelve looked remarkably like sisters or relatives, though they were of different families, and she grouped these together. The other five didn't really fit the profile she was developing but she tacked them up anyways — not wanting to leave one child behind. Printing these pictures from the microfiche negatives made the girls faces look like ghostly, x-ray scans, and it unnerved her a little — like they were already dead. She gave a silent prayer for their safe return, like the six she had rescued. But in her heart, with all the years that had passed, she feared the worst.

Next, she dug out one of Bill's state maps and set pins at the addresses of each girl.

Then, since Samuel/Tony was her only lead, she pinned all the areas he had lived, worked, or visited that she knew about. That meant his old residence with Janet, Larson's various properties, Smithson's Lake, and her motel. Adding the final pin into her motel's location gave her the creeps. But overlaying these locations didn't help her case against Samuel any. Only three girls lived near his and Janet's old apartment, another girl was from a farm close to a Larson property that was raided for its financial records, and the rest weren't even close. Without a complete record of where he travelled, Mabel couldn't tell what sort of associations he had with them.

Her gaze fell back to the pin over her diner and motel.

It drew her in, and she touched it.

Then she had an inspiration.

She rushed out of her office and straight to her bedroom closet. Then she dove into a box where she kept her father's old worn motel guest ledgers. Written in his hand, she had kept them for sentimental reasons, a reminder to treat guests like kin, as he had.

Her dad started the motel in 1945 from a GI loan after his wartime stint in Italy and France, and his records were meticulous. Sitting cross-legged on the floor, she searched the guest lists, paying attention to the tourist season months. She started at the beginning and was about to give up by the time she found it.

Ms. Kerns and Son, July 10-17, 1952.

She stared at the entry.

Then shivered.

Samuel and his mother had stayed at the motel when he was a child.

Mabel recalled how terrible that summer was. Her dog had been killed by some wild animal. She had found him dead out back, poor thing, before she had run crying to her dad, who came out and took care of the remains. To this day, a cross still marks where they buried him, and she never wanted another dog since, despite pleas from her boys.

As the child of parents who ran a motel and diner in a remote mountain town, Mabel's childhood was unusual. The kids who stayed at the motel often became her friends. Her father had even set up a swing set and sandbox at the back of the motel where Mabel's boys still played. She recalled spending hours and hours playing there with the tourist kids, and she had even stayed in touch with several of them to this day. Mabel's mother enjoyed taking photographs back then and would often take pictures of Mabel and the guests, especially the children and—

The negatives.

Mabel rushed down to the basement and hunted through the dusty boxes until she found her mother's effects. Her mom had taken thousands of photo negatives and kept detailed records, just like her husband. Mabel grabbed the box containing the negatives from 1950 to 1960 and hauled them upstairs to her bedroom.

Dropping it on her bed, she went back to searching the guest ledgers and discovered that Angelica and her son had visited four summers in a row. In one entry, for 1953, Angelica had even listed her son's name — Samuel.

Another piece of the puzzle fell into place.

She searched through years of her mother's negatives, holding them up to her desk lamp. Finally, she found something from 1955, around the time Angelica and Samuel had stayed at the motel — a series of Mabel playing with the tourist kids. There was a negative of Mabel and her mother laughing and swinging on a swing set, one obviously taken by her dad. But the grainy image included a blonde-haired woman and a boy about ten, standing nearby and watching them. It was hard to pick out the details, so she used various magnifying lenses to make them out. The middle-aged woman looked like a younger, morose Angelica, and the frowning boy beside her must be Samuel.

Could a killer have stayed here when he was young?

She pressed her hand to her chest to steady her thumping heart, but her hand started fluttering too.

Could the killer be coming to the diner even now?

CHAPTER 20

Monday, October 12, 1987

Two weeks later, Mabel sat down with a cup of tea to pour over her notes and recollections. After that night in the office, she'd set her mind on meeting with each missing girl's family, a task that required careful scheduling around diner shifts and her own family's needs and many miles driving to all corners of the state.

With each mother met, each girl's story learned, Mabel's heart broke a little bit more. For each troubled past, there were happy moments shared. But for all the mothers there was guilt — for surviving, for not doing enough, for old arguments, for not being better to their child. Each mother had assumed they would have time to repair their relationships, but now they were left with only memories, guilt, and shame. By the end of it, Mabel didn't think she could cry anymore.

After the first few nights of the family interviews, she would come home and hug her boys for no reason other than to show them her love. As the days progressed, her patience waned, and she often scolded them for small things that normally wouldn't bother her. And by the end, she simply collapsed in her rocking chair, wanting only a glass of wine and silence. If it wasn't for Bill, rubbing her feet on the couch or giving her a back rub in bed, she couldn't have done it. He was gentle and patient and took on more of the parenting duties as her focus was elsewhere. Even his issues with Walter and the trade show seemed to be in the past. If it weren't for her being so emotionally wreaked by hearing sad stories from the families of the missing girls, this would have been a happier time for her and her family. But instead, she was feeling her own guilt and shame. Guilt for not doing enough for the missing girls, guilt for still having her children, and guilt for not spending enough time with them.

But she'd found another clue.

The son of the Andersons — the twelfth family she had visited — had seen an older man with his sister. He had drawn a sketch for police, but it hadn't ended up in the paper. It showed a middle-aged white man with a mustache and a ball cap. Mabel thought at first it was Samuel, but the face was generic enough it could have been almost anyone. She borrowed it to make a photocopy at a local library and added it to her evidence collection.

Mabel set down her tea and scanned her wall board, with no real idea of what to do next. Calling individual police departments had gotten her nowhere. Mostly she was shunted around various departments until she landed on the right detectives, who either had no initial recollection of the case or told her flat out to stay out of it.

She got up and unpinned the business card of FBI agent John Ford, recalling his offer to provide advice. She certainly needed it now. It was close to six o'clock, but she dialed him anyway, fully expecting to reach an answering machine.

About to give up after the fourth ring, Mabel was surprised when his voice came on the line. "BSU. John Ford speaking."

Mabel nearly dropped the phone. "John!" she burst out, her voice louder than normal.

"Um, yes? No need to shout, ma'am."

"Oh sorry. This is Mabel. Mabel Davison."

His silence made her realize he probably didn't remember her, so she added in a rush, "I met you at the Monroe prison, and I, um, was interviewing Karl Larson."

"Oh yes, of course. Nice to speak to you again, Ms. Davison. What can I do for you?"

"Excuse me for being so flustered, but I need your advice. About the missing girls' cases."

"Oh," he replied, sounding a little hesitant. "My unit deals with serial murderers, not trafficking or runaways. I'm not sure how much I can be of help for that."

"No, I mean, yes. I think these girls could have been murdered."

"Think? Or do you know for certain?"

"Honestly," she sighed. "I don't know." She looked at the photos on her wall. "Larson had this house of horrors where he abducted girls, got them hooked on drugs, and then abused them. Six girls were rescued, but there's at least seventeen more missing since '79 and it's been so long I think that the FBI could be right. That they were murdered."

"What's the link between all these girls?"

"They all look strikingly similar, were all taken around the western region of the state, and most had come from poor families."

"How do you know they were taken?"

"I talked to the families. Well, most of them. None of the mothers believe their girls ran away. And I got a lead. A drawing of a man — a suspect, I mean."

"What does he look like?"

"A middle-aged white man with a mustache, ball cap and, um … that's it." She winced, a little embarrassed by how generic it was, fearing he would just brush her off.

But when he spoke, he sounded interested. "In my cases, generic is actually pretty normal. Were the victims all white too?"

"How did you know?"

"Serial killers don't usually kill outside their race."

"Oh, and I have a name for my suspect too."

"Wow. Okay, who is it?"

"A Tony Ketch — well, he was born Samuel, but he uses his father's name now. He's in his forties and has a mustache."

"Why him?"

"Well," Mabel took a deep breath to organize her thoughts. "First off, Larson didn't start that horrid place where he held the girls. But he told me Tony did."

"Do you trust what he says? Larson, I mean."

"Well, no," Mabel admitted. "But I don't think he's lying."

John paused like he was thinking it through. "I was debating whether to expand our study of serial murderers to mafia and drug bosses, but I haven't done it yet. I can't say I'm convinced this isn't a trafficking case. Are there any bodies?"

"Um … no."

"It's outside my jurisdiction then. You've done some great work here, really, but we can't discount some other trafficking ring or that these girls simply ran off on their own."

"But that's not what their mothers think."

"That's not enough for a judge, Ms. Davison. You need hard evidence," John said, then paused. "Were any of the missing girls near where your suspect lived or worked?" Mabel told him about the few ties she knew. "Do you know anything about the suspect's family?" Mabel told him about how controlling Angelica was and that his father died when he was young.

"Good. You've done your homework. Most detectives don't bother with the family history, but that's turning into a significant part of how we do our profiles. Do you know where the girls were last seen?"

"No, not really. Some were on their way to school, others going to or from a mall. But I can't find any patterns."

"And you don't know where the murder sites or drop off sites are because there are no bodies," John stated then paused. "No. Sorry. I can't do it until there is at least one body, preferably more. Serial killers often go back and visit their kill or abduction sites. It's either about sexual stimulation or control or both. They like to remember and relive the experiences. It energizes them."

Mabel absorbed this advice as John took a moment. "Anything else about the mother? You said she was controlling. Were there any places they went to together? Any place that might be nostalgic for him? For example, where was the first girl abducted?"

"Tacoma," Mabel said. "He lived there with his girlfriend at the same time. But ... I've got to be honest here. The girlfriend doesn't think my suspect could have done it. She says he was kind to her and wouldn't harm a soul. Does that mean I'm wrong to suspect him?"

"That he had a girlfriend? No. That's not why. That she doesn't think he's capable of it is not entirely unusual either. What we are finding is that while, yes, some of these killers are loners, most have a girlfriend or even are married with children. These men want to blend in. Fit in. You described him as generic looking, and that doesn't bother me. It almost fits. These men are good at covering their tracks, being meticulous, and disappearing in plain sight."

"Janet said he worked till late at night sometimes. He visited a strip club here in Blue River. That's where Larson's upper management had meetings, or so she thought, but he always came back sober."

"If he wasn't there, he could have been hunting," John replied. "These men hunt for targets, and they don't act on their urges until they are certain that they won't be discovered. One subject I interviewed said he had no problem going out to hunt at least thirty or forty times before finding the right victim. This is partly why they aren't easily caught. They are expert killers who develop patterns and procedures to avoid detection. Even though most have sexual control fantasies, they are meticulous and deliberate until the act. Then they're quite brutal, I'm afraid, and often take mementos of the crimes. If there's any place that was special to him, start there. That's all I can say."

"Alright," Mabel said, sounding more disappointed than she felt.

"Hang in there, Mabel. Sounds like you found some good evidence already. If there's a break in the case, call me. And if not, I don't mind giving advice. That's part of my job. I'm here to teach local law enforcement about what to look for."

"I'm a private investigator, luv."

"All the same," he said, then made his goodbye.

Energized from his praise and encouragement, Mabel took her time examining the map on her wallboard, scanning all the pins marking Samuel's known locations. Then she stopped to stare at the pin over Smithson Lake.

CHAPTER 21

Wednesday, October 14, 1987

With the kids at school and Bill off at the hardware store in Tacoma, Mabel grabbed Kerry's old hiking boots and a warm jacket and drove to the place off the highway where the locals parked before walking the short, forested trail to Smithson Lake.

A fall frost had lightly coated the pines and chilled the air enough to see her breath. Unused to hiking, she was tired by the time she made it to the lonely lake.

The crystalline blue waters, not yet frozen, reflected the vast mountain and snow-tipped trees beyond. A short wooden bridge connected the lake's small island to its picturesque shore. The lake was frequented by weekend party goers, who often came here to build campfires on its beaches or within the island's grove.

Mabel avoided the popular spots and walked the lake's edge, finding herself scanning the forest for any signs of disturbance.

But the woods stretched on for miles and were so thick that even just a few dozen feet inside the treeline remained hidden. Disappointed, she slowed and then stopped to rest on a frost-covered drift log, barren of bark, white like bone.

Staring at the calm waters caused her to sum her efforts these past few months — the name of a suspect based on the word of a drug lord and nothing more. And with the passing of time since the abductions, her investigation felt more like a recovery of bodies than an opportunity for rescue. She picked up a rock and threw it angrily at the water, and the splash echoed farther than it should before the sound cut off sharply.

A heavy silence followed.

Not even a raven cawed.

The sheer weight of it bent her head and her breathing became labored. Then the skin on the back of her neck prickled and her eyes widened.

She whirled around.

But no one was there in the dark spaces between the pines.

CHAPTER 22

Thursday to Friday, November 5-6, 1987

S everal weeks had passed, during which Mabel had made it a habit to hike around the lake, often peering into the woods for any sign of a grave. The frost hadn't returned, but it was getting cooler again and she wore a heavy sweater or jacket. Sometimes Bill and the kids would join her on the hikes without knowing the reason, and they would stop and play by the beach. But her mind was on darker things, wondering if any of the girls had been buried out there.

Bill had joined her this afternoon trying to make it romantic, but with her focused on the case, she grew cross with him. When they returned home, a chastened Bill headed to the den to watch an Afterschool Special on TV with the kids while she checked in on the diner, more to get away from her family than anything else.

Dan was at the counter, rooted to his favorite stool and deep into his Thursday paperwork. A couple diners passing by said hi to him, which he only gruffly acknowledged. Not the friendliest of sheriffs, she thought once again, but his heart was in the right place.

Mabel put on her apron and, without his asking, served him a piece of pie and an extra scoop of ice cream. He brightened and took a bite. And with her case always top of mind, she asked without any preamble, "How do you search for a body in the forest?"

Dan nearly choked and took a moment to swallow. "Jeez Mabel! That's a strange thing to ask on a Thursday night."

"I'm serious."

"You thinkin' of them girls again, I reckon. Maybe them coming to an untimely end?"

She looked away. "Yes. Maybe. I don't know. But after all this time since their abductions, I'm…" she sighed, "losing hope."

Dan nodded like he had expected her to say that.

He stuck his fork upright into his pie and took his time to wipe his mouth. "Well," he said finally. "The short answer is dogs, of course. Fortunately, Kennie and I got a buddy we hunt with and his dogs are always picking up a scent. If he takes his pack down to the lake, he'll find what you're looking for."

"Would he do that?"

Dan pursed his lips, thinking about it. "I reckon, I guess. Craig owes me since I gave him a really good cut of moose meat, seeing as I bagged my quota this year and that poor sod can't shoot worth a dam." He pointed to the phone. "Hand me that blower there." He told her the number to dial and she handed the receiver over.

Dan said gruffly into the phone, "Craig. Yep. Need you and your dogs tomorrow. No. Not a hunt. We're going to Smithson Lake to look for some bodies. Okay, see you tomorrow. 3 PM?" Dan looked at Mabel and she nodded. "3 PM." Then Dan handed back the receiver and went back to eating his pie.

Mabel asked, "Didn't he want to know *why* we're looking for bodies?"

Dan shrugged and kept eating.

"Okay then," Mabel said, turning away stunned but also a little amused, wondering what she was getting herself into.

* * *

The following afternoon Dan and Mabel arrived at the same time at the gravel parking lot off the highway near Smithson Lake. Craig was already there, prepping his dogs.

When she handed Dan a thermos and a sandwich, he gestured for her to come closer and whispered, "Don't say nothing about the size of them dogs. He's a little sensitive."

Mabel whispered back. "Why dachshunds? I was expecting bloodhounds or something."

"That's why he's sensitive. But his critters can sniff out a deer, boar, badgers, above ground, underground. All good," Dan said, as he brought her to his friend.

Craig was a tall man with a slight build and messy, sandy hair. He wore forest-patterned camouflage and combat boots and was at least ten years younger than both Dan and Mabel. He responded to Mabel's cheerful greeting with a serious, silent nod and Mabel could see why these two probably got along so well.

Craig asked Dan, "We looking for bodies?"

"Yep."

"Fresh or drowned?"

Dan glanced at Mabel, who didn't know how to answer that. "Planted, I expect. Maybe what? Three to five years?"

Mabel nodded.

"Any clothes or such they can track a scent on?" Craig asked her.

Dan cut in, "Just what God gave us today." Then he turned to Mabel, hitched up his belt, and said, "Best you go back to the diner and leave it to us men. Craig's going to be running up and down them woods while I'll man the main path to keep us on track."

"Sounds good to me," Mabel said, happy to leave them to it, handing Craig the last thermos and sandwich.

Craig's flat expression finally cracked a smile at the gift of food. "That's mighty Christian of you. Rest assured, if something's out there, we'll find it." Then he turned to his dogs, grasped their long leashes tighter, and shouted, "Killer, Bandit, Badger, Snowball, go, go, go!"

Craig's pack of barking, small dogs dragged him off into the woods while Dan whooped and chased after them.

Mabel couldn't help but laugh at the sight. Not having much faith about this whole adventure, she decided to trust Dan and head back home before she went to work.

* * *

Back at the diner, Mabel put on her apron and was about to flip through the remaining orders when Molly drew closer, put her back to the seated customers, and whispered, "We got a strange one."

Mabel scanned the diner, as Molly continued, "He's alone in the back booth. Been sitting there an hour. Doesn't talk. Just drinks coffee and writes in some journal."

Mabel laughed. "What's wrong with that?"

"Nothing wrong per se. It's just the look about him. The way he looks at you … like he's angry or mean or something. I don't know. I've never seen such a look in someone's eyes like that, and he keeps looking over at the Wilson girls for some reason."

Mabel frowned. Amber and Allison, the 16-year-old Wilson twins, often hung out at the diner after school, like today when their mom had errands to do in town.

Mabel could see how the man was staring at them over a sip of coffee.

He was about forty, with a ball cap and mustache, wearing a long trench coat though it was warm inside. He had a pair of gloves and a small kit of some sort on the table beside him.

Mabel told Molly she'd take care of it and then went about refilling coffee cups while keeping an eye on him. Whether he was drinking his coffee or writing in a small notebook, his gaze kept returning to the girls. Mabel's disgust at an older man leering at these teen girls made the momma-bear part of her mad.

Having enough of it now, she strode over and stood beside him, coffee pot in hand.

He avoided her by reading his journal.

She cleared her throat loudly.

Finally, he looked up, but his glare was so menacing that Mabel stepped back, realizing why Molly was so put off.

"You want some coffee, *sir*?"

He shook his head like he didn't want to be disturbed. Then glanced over at the teen girls again. Mabel tracked his gaze to confirm who he was looking at and then said firmly, "Looks like you've had your fill then. I'd say your time here is over. You should pack up your things."

The man glanced up again, startled. "You're asking me to leave?" His malevolent undertone was something she'd expect from Larson's old gang — not her customers.

She nodded, stepping back to give him a path out and to put some space between them.

He grumbled and took his time to consider it before he huffed, gathered his things, and got up. His dark eyes stared deep into hers and there was an evilness to them that she hadn't seen before but for Larson. As her heart started to pound, she had a revelation. This could be her suspect. This could be Samuel!

Her throat constricted and she couldn't get his name out as he stepped so close she could smell the coffee on his breath. She moved backward a half-step, folding her arms across her chest but stopped there — this was her place, and she wasn't going to back down. He gave her a hesitant, cold once-over before he turned, glanced at the girls, and then stalked out the door.

Mabel rushed to a window to spy what car he was driving.

Then as the man drove off, Sheriff Dan's cruiser rolled in, and Mabel ran out to meet him. Dan rolled down the window. "What's up? I can tell you how it went inside."

"No! Not that! It's him, Dan! It's him!"

"Who?"

"I think it's Samuel! The man I've been tracking. Samuel Ketch! He was staring at the Wilson girls. I think he was hunting, Dan. That's what the FBI said. He was hunting girls!"

Dan's startled, perplexed look gave way to a fierceness. He tipped his hat and backed up his cruiser. Then as he turned onto the highway, his flashing lights blinked a streaking red and blue, and he raced after the car.

Mabel went back into the diner and shouted at Molly about to clear off his table, "Hold on a sec!"

Mabel grabbed a pair of gloves behind the counter. "Evidence," she explained, then carefully put the coffee mug onto a tray for the DNA — just like when she had tracked Lee Wallach. Proud like she had somehow stopped a major crime.

Twenty minutes later, Dan's cruiser rolled back into the lot but with the back seat empty. A concerned Mabel waited at the door for Dan to amble in and take off his hat.

"Did he escape?"

Dan gave her a look. "About that." He tossed his hat on the counter. "I pulled him over. But I can't arrest a man for drinking coffee."

"But he was hunting Amber and Allison!" Mabel pointed to the Wilson twins, who stared back like startled does, so Mabel lowered her voice. "That's what the FBI said. These men hunt women, little girls. He was staring at them!"

"Look. A man looking at girls, however old, ain't a crime. If I had to make arrests for a man ogling a woman, half the men in town would be in jail."

"Well, don't you find that just a little creepy?"

Dan made a face as he reconsidered it and then nodded, chastened. "Still, when I pulled him over, he seemed normal enough. Polite. Friendly. Hell, I wish most of my stops were so easy."

"I'm investigating him for murder or abducting girls. Why else would Samuel show up here?"

"Well," Dan drawled out. "That's another thing. It ain't him. I pulled over a Mr. Paul Hammetts, who lives in Tacoma. He said he just needed to clear his head after a fight with his wife and he wanted to get out of the house and write out his thoughts. I don't understand the writing part, but the rest checks out."

"Are you sure?"

"I know a fake license when I see it. His was legit. He ain't your man."

"Well, are you going to call his wife? Make sure his alibi is legitimate?"

Dan scoffed. "No. Why would I?"

Mabel lifted her palms up in frustration.

"Okay. Alright," Dan said. "I got the man's details. When I go home later, I'll check in on his wife and see if he made it home, deal? I worked up too much an appetite chasing them dogs around Smithson to do it now."

Mabel gave him a look, knowing he was only trying to change the subject, so she wagged her finger at him. "You better call later." Then she gave in and asked, lamely, "I suppose you want something to eat before we talk?"

Dan smiled.

"I imagine a beer, too?" she asked with some sass to make it clear she wasn't happy.

"That's it," Dan said, pointing to her as he settled in his stool. Then as she got the beer, he said, "Craig and

I run up and down them hills many times." Mabel doubted how much running Dan did. "And it was tiring, I tells ya. But we searched all over and his dogs found nothing. Excepting if you consider an old tire, a boot, and a broken shovel evidence. No bodies. No burials. Nothing."

"Well, they aren't bloodhounds."

Dan looked firmly at her. "I seen them dogs track a badger scent for a mile, then dive deep into a hole I wouldn't have thought was there and kill that critter in its den. Them dogs can sniff a game trail that's for sure. It was them dogs that sniffed out that moose for me, which is why I gave Craig some of the share. Them dogs ain't the problem." Dan grabbed the beer and then settled in closer to the television set. "There are no bodies at Smithson Lake." He tipped the beer in thanks before settling in to watch CBS sports.

"Burger's ready," Kevin called out from the kitchen.

Without knowing what else to say, she grabbed the burger and a water pitcher and walked around the counter. She touched Dan's shoulder as she dropped his meal off to let him know she appreciated his efforts and put on a brave face for the Wilson girls while filling their glasses, but inwardly she was mad.

She hadn't protected anyone tonight, had treated a customer poorly, and was nowhere near solving the case. Her one lead — Samuel — was looking like a dead end, and the mothers of those missing girls were probably crying themselves to sleep tonight. Again.

Fuming, she swept up the tray with Mr. Hammetts' coffee cup and plate and then went into the kitchen and dumped it all into the industrial sink, shattering the dishes into pieces.

CHAPTER 23

Thursday, November 12, 1987

A week later, Mabel was wiping the diner counter when Kevin came out of the kitchen. "Did you take a case of beer out of the walk-in? My count's off."

"No. But maybe Molly did," Mabel replied.

"Nope. Already asked her. And a few bottles haven't been getting logged recently, which happens, but an entire case now? I'm scratching my head. I don't know, maybe I just messed up."

"Let me double-check the log, dear."

Sure enough, Kevin's signature marked the right number from the shipment and when she went back to the storage room and counted, it was a case short. She frowned.

"Sorry, Mabel," Kevin said.

"Oh, no, dear. It's fine. It's probably me," she replied, smiling through her concern.

Stepping out into the diner, she stopped short to look out the windows at her home. Bill would be there now, she thought. She turned to go home and ask him about this, but the phone rang, dragging her back to the counter. She answered distractedly, "Mabel's Diner and Motel. Your home away from home."

"Mabel!" Dan yelled, breathless.

"What is it now?"

"We found one!"

"Found one what?"

"A body! We found a body!"

Mabel grasped the counter to steady herself as she asked, "At Smithson's Lake?"

"No. Leavenworth!" Leavenworth was a small town about twenty miles from Blue River. "I mean, just outside it in the woods. Staties are all over it. A man with his dogs was checking out an old Larson farm for sale in that upcoming state auction when one of his dogs brings back a bone — a human leg bone! Staties taped off the crime scene and brought in forensics. Even the media are flocking there like a pack of buzzards. Kennie's there to keep back the crowd and he tells me that bone's been in the woods for years. I told him you were looking for a body. And now one is found!"

"Leavenworth? I don't know if Samuel was there."

"Maybe it wasn't him. But this could be related to your case!" Dan shouted, excited. "I'm going to head out. And no, Mabel, you can't go out there too. Stay put and I'll give you more details as soon as I can."

Mabel put down the receiver slowly. Her mind flickered back to the September visit she'd had with Patty, whose daughter Sandra had disappeared four years ago. She pictured Patty getting a knock on her front door from police officers, hats in hands, asking to come in, and Patty backing away, hands covering her mouth, realizing her worst nightmare was about to come true.

She willed herself not to cry. But she thought about Patty and Sandra all day while refilling coffees and taking orders. Every time the phone rang, or the bell chimed above the door, her heart skipped a beat, thinking it was Dan with news. At about 3 o'clock, a man in his thirties walked in, carrying a notebook, and went straight to her.

He read her nametag and smiled. "My names Bob Hackett," he said, reaching out to shake her hand a little too long. "Nice to meet the famous Mabel."

"Oh?" She pulled her hand back.

"Your name's on the sign, right?"

"Oh, of course." She relaxed and then added with a slight curtsy, "Yours truly."

"Can I grab a seat?"

"Anywhere you like, hon."

He laid out his notebook and pen and sat at the counter while she poured him a cup of coffee.

"Are you a bird watcher?"

"Something like that," he said, smiling while taking a sip. "Ah, that's good." Then when she was about to serve the main room, he gestured for her to stay a moment. "Hey, I hear you're a PI too."

"Excuse me?"

"I heard you solved a couple of big cases. That's interesting."

Mabel breathed out. "Oh, I didn't have that big of a role."

"Really? That's not what I was told. You helped rescue your niece and took down the notorious Karl Larson. That's impressive."

"Oh, I'm just glad it happened," Mabel replied, a little thrown by this stranger's knowledge and brushing him off. "All I did was go down to a farm and get my niece back and call the police."

Bob wrote what she said in his notebook. "Amazing. Yeah, the abduction is why the FBI was involved, but it was the DEA's raid. I heard there was a confidential informant, and that was you, right?"

"Well, I'm…" She paused, as he was writing her words again. "Excuse me, what are you doing?"

"Taking notes. I'm a journalist. Didn't I mention that?"

"No. I—I don't think so. And I don't think I want to be interviewed."

"Sure, sure. Wasn't it true that you were almost a victim of the Thompson killers?" he asked, impressed. "Man, that must have been scary all alone with them in a sawmill at night, right?"

"I really don't want to talk about it."

"Okay. Let's go back to the body then. Out in Leavenworth. How did you know a girl would be found there? The forensics team's first thoughts are foul play."

Mabel's hand fluttered to her heart, shocked that one of her missing girls was truly dead. She stammered, "A girl? I—I didn't know that till now. Did you talk to Dan?"

"Who's Dan?" he asked, writing the name down.

"I don't think we should talk about this."

"It's all good. Don't worry. I have a source at the crime scene on record. You can talk to me, it's okay. So, tell me, how did you know the girl would be found on a Larson property? Do you know her name?"

Mabel backed away, flustered, and a hovering Molly rushed to her side. "Who are you?" Molly demanded.

"Bob Hackett, *Seattle Times*," the reporter replied before turning back to Mabel. "If you can confirm that you were the DEA informant on the Larson case, that'll be worth my trip."

"Actually," Molly cut in. "I think we're done."

"I only have a few more questions."

"She said no."

Bob ignored Molly and kept his attention on Mabel. "You *were* the DEA's informant, weren't you? Yes? Or no? You can nod if you want."

"She said no," Molly repeated forcefully. "You need to leave."

Bob looked at Mabel. "If you want to talk, give me a call. Here." He pulled out a card to hand it to her.

Molly grabbed it instead. "She'll call you if she wants to. But this is over for you. Now!"

"You're going to be part of this story, whether you like it or not. Talk to me and you can get ahead of it all. You don't have much time. Other reporters are coming and they might not be as nice." He rapped the counter with his knuckles to emphasize his point and left.

Mabel watched as he got into his car, still shocked that the press was involved. Being interviewed was the last thing she wanted. That's why Lavi always spoke to the reporters, allowing her to remain anonymous. Until now.

Molly hugged her. "Don't you worry. He's gone now."

The phone rang and Mabel nearly jumped. Molly answered and then gave the receiver over to Mabel. "It's Dan."

Mabel paused to collect herself before she asked, weakly, "Yes?"

"Watch out," Dan growled. "Press here are asking all sorts of questions. A dang rookie on the forensics team gave your name to a *Seattle Times* reporter. I'm sorry Mabel. If any reporters come by, just tell 'em nothing, or tell them to go take a hike."

Mabel squeezed her aching temples. "One was here already. He asked me all sorts of questions."

"You didn't answer him, did you?"

"No. Yes! Well, I mean I did. At the start. But that was before I knew he was a journalist and Molly made him leave."

"Ugh, don't talk to any others. Please. Once the press knows, everything changes."

Mabel cursed herself for even speaking to Bob. But then she thought of something worse. "Are they going to tell the parents first? Before this gets out in the papers?"

"Can't. We don't know who the vic is. It's all bones and tattered women's clothes, so forensics'll be examining it. They'll have to identify the poor thing through dental records, personal effects, missing person cases that sort of thing. But the first pass is that she was in her teens and was planted within a few winters in these woods."

Mabel's voice broke with despair. "But all the parents will wonder. They'll know a young girl has been murdered. They just won't know if it's their daughter or not."

"Afraid so."

Mabel pressed her fingers deeper into her forehead and squeezed her eyes shut.

"Now don't you go crying on me and feeling all guilty about this."

Tears burst out of her, and she felt stupid for them. "I gotta go," she said quickly before hanging up.

Molly was beside her. "You should go home."

Mabel nodded, overwhelmed as Molly briefly hugged her then stepped away to attend to a customer.

The phone rang again, and Mabel collected herself enough to answer it, presuming it was Dan. "I'm okay. I promise—"

"—This is Betty Peterson of the *Tacoma News*. Is a Mabel Davison there?"

"She's not here," Mabel replied quickly before slamming the receiver down, frightened.

Molly rushed back. "What happened? Was that Dan?"

The phone started ringing again.

"Don't answer it!" Mabel nearly shouted before forcing herself to sound calmer. "I … It's the press. I'm … I'm going home. Just tell them … I'm not here or something."

"What if they stop by?"

Mabel groaned inwardly. "Please don't send them to my house. I need some time. To think."

"Of course, dear. I'll hold down the fort. Go get some rest."

Mabel nodded and then slowly took off her nametag and apron, but when the phone rang again, she threw them in a drawer and fled out the door. Behind her, Molly answered, "Mabel's Diner and Motel. A home away from—"

CHAPTER 24

Friday, November 13, 1987

Normally, Mabel didn't read the newspapers she provided her customers, but today a concerned-looking Molly gave Mabel a big hug at the start of her morning shift before handing her one and telling her to read it.

Dollhouse Killer Strikes Twice!

Mabel covered her mouth and slowly took a seat, reading the article. As Dan had told her, the human remains were believed to be several years old and likely from a teenage girl. But her horror grew as she learned that another girl's body had been found nearby, this one having been left far more recently. Investigators at the scene said the girl was wearing garishly applied makeup, a white wig and had brightly painted fingernails.

Mabel's gut twisted. Then she froze.

Her name was in the paper too.

"Oh no," she groaned. Bob Hackett had made her out to be some sort of hero-citizen investigating crimes. But he incorrectly reported that she had been searching for the missing girls around Leavenworth. He described her role in catching Karen Thompson's killers and taking down the Larson drug operation, and implied that she was a DEA informant.

She slammed the paper down, furious.

Molly came closer and said, awed, "I didn't know you told the police where to search."

"I did no such thing!" Mabel fumed. "That Hackett implied that I did something here. I did nothing. He even quoted me wrong, for Pete's sake."

"But that's not how it reads in the paper. And he said such nice things about you!"

"Ugh, I guess you can't believe everything you read in the papers," Mabel said, shaking her head. Then touched Molly's arm. "Please don't mention this. It's those poor girls and their mothers that we should be thinking of."

Molly nodded and stepped away while Mabel stewed, feeling like she'd either scream from Hackett's outing her or tear her hair out about those poor girls. Usually, at the start of a shift, any concerns faded away as she focused on making her customers happy. Now, she didn't want to be here. She swept up her nametag and roughly pinned it near her heart. She caught an old man staring at her before he quickly hid under his newspaper, and Mabel's shoulders sagged.

The door chime rang, and she willed herself to put on a friendly face for her new customers, but her smile fell as a man and woman, both wearing suits, walked directly to her, one of them flashing a badge.

"Detective Sue Tomlinson, State Police," the serious-looking woman said.

"Detective Todd Smith," her partner added. He was taller than Detective Tomlinson, had a leaner athletic build, and a friendlier smile. "We just have some questions for you, ma'am."

Mabel saw her customers look up from their newspapers so she replied in an overly loud voice so they could overhear. "I want you to know that I had nothing to do with what's in the paper. That was wrong."

"We don't read the papers, ma'am. But we've heard from the sheriff's office that you might have some information to share."

Mabel's face turned beet red, and she gave in, feeling the heat of everyone's stares. "Let's find a private place to talk."

As Mabel led the detectives outside, she said, "I had nothing to do with finding those girls in Leavenworth. The sheriff must have told you about what I'm doing and maybe the ones found could be the girls I'm looking for."

Detective Sue Tomlinson glanced at her partner before asking Mabel, "Are you some sort of concerned citizen, then?"

"I have a private investigator's license."

"Can we see it?" Detective Todd Smith asked. "And your license to carry."

"Carry what, luv?"

"Guns. Firearms."

"Oh, sorry, no. I don't believe in guns."

"Really?" he sounded doubtful. "We can check on that."

"Well, please do," Mabel replied, a little irritated.

Mabel then led them into her home and took off her shoes while the detectives didn't, tracking wet prints into the den. "My office is upstairs," she said, ignoring the mess she'd have to clean later, redirecting them upstairs. The male detective lagged half-a-step behind, peeking into the bedrooms as they passed, while Detective Tomlinson kept pace with Mabel.

"Who lives with you?"

"I have two boys. Twelve and nine. And my husband, Bill."

"Do they know the two deceased girls?"

"I don't even know who they are," Mabel replied weakly, leading her into the office filled with her evidence.

Detective Tomlinson stopped short as her mouth dropped.

Her partner came in around her. "Woah!" he added. Then he whistled thinly as he scanned the wallboard filled with the photocopies of the missing girls' microfiche pictures, the marked-up map, and Mabel's notes and printouts.

"You did all this?"

Mabel nodded.

Detective Tomlinson pointed to one of the pictures for her partner's benefit — it was Sandra Hoffman.

Mabel asked, "Oh my God, is it her?"

"What information do you have on this one?"

"Quite a bit," Mabel replied, a little proud that she could help in spite of the situation. She tapped different points on the wallboard, as she explained, "I have the news stories on their disappearances here, my interviews of the parents there, and these photos, of course."

Detective Tomlinson pointed to the drawing of her suspect. "What's this?"

"The Anderson's son saw a white man, mid-40s, mustache, hanging out with their daughter. He made that drawing and I think it's of a man named Samuel Ke—"

"Who're the Andersons?" Detective Tomlinson cut her off. But her partner followed closely with, "I heard you're a contractor for the public defender's office."

"The Andersons have a missing girl here," Mabel pointed out the photo to answer the first question. Then Mabel turned to Detective Smith. "I was originally helping Lavi, that's Mr. Arronson, find Candy Johnson's daughter. During that time, I discovered these girls here were missing too. I had some leads, but it wasn't until my niece got taken that—"

"We know the Larson case."

"Well, okay. But you probably don't know that these girls" — Mabel pointed to Sandra and Tracy — "were still missing after that. And none of Larson's associates said anything about them until I spoke to Kyle, this man here, who told me about this Samuel Ketch I was about to mention. He's linked to Larson too and—"

"Any link to this girl?" Detective Tomlinson pointed to Sandra again.

Mabel hesitated. "Well, you can see how similar these girls are."

"No, I mean, can you tie him to her?"

"Like I said, they look similar. And are all the same ages, coming from multiple areas—"

"We've got two bodies. You're saying someone murdered … how many on this wall, ten, twenty?"

"Eighteen," Detective Smith cut in and answered.

"It's actually seventeen," Mabel said, defensive. "That I know of. And I have here in my notes that—"

"Can we take these?"

"What? My notes?"

Detective Smith started unpinning them, plus the photos of Sandra. "This wall map … does it have the spots where they were abducted?"

"No, just where they live."

He left it as is. Then he folded her notes and photos in half and Mabel was going to ask him to stop bending them like that when his partner stepped in. "Can we see your license, ma'am?"

"What? Oh, okay," Mabel replied, flustered. She started searching her desk but couldn't find it and felt even more embarrassed when she caught a snide glance between the two detectives. She found the card and proudly showed them.

"Mr. Arronson hired you for" — Detective Tomlinson waved at the board — "this?"

"No. He's not part of it. I'm doing it on my own."

Detective Tomlinson made a face like she tasted something bitter. "Why?"

"Like I said, these two girls are missing, and their mothers have a right to know. The others I just found out about."

Detective Tomlinson threw a long look at her partner before turning back to Mabel, her face dead serious. "Ma'am, I cannot stress enough that this is a police investigation. We don't need nosy citizens poking into our cases. In my experience, it causes more harm than good. Have you visited the Leavenworth site?" Mabel shook her head. "And never met these girls in person before they were taken?"

"No, but I met their families recently."

"And talked to the press," Detective Tomlinson muttered.

"I didn't mean to. I thought that Bob Hackett was just a customer, not a journalist."

"Well, don't next time. This isn't gossip, this is serious."

"But I didn't—"

Detective Tomlinson cut her off to ask her partner, "You have any more questions?"

He nodded. "The local sheriff said there was a man…" He flipped open his notebook. "A Paul Hammetts. The sheriff pulled him over based on your complaint."

"Well yes, but Dan said he was—"

"He's a known sexual deviant."

"A what?"

"A pedophile. Goes after young girls, that sort of thing. He's on a watch list for this area. Why did you ask the sheriff to pull him over?"

Mabel put her hand to her chest, overwhelmed by their questions. "H-he was looking funny at the Wilson girls. They're sixteen."

The detectives exchanged glances. "Can you give us their names?" Mabel did. "Do you have any contact information for the Wilson family?"

"The girls come to my diner now and then, and I know the family fairly well, but we don't call each other. They're in the phone book."

Detective Smith wrote a note in his little booklet. "You said you saw him leering at these girls, then called the sheriff, right?"

"Well, yes and no. Dan was stopping by as he had gone to Smithson Lake with some tracking dogs for me and—"

"He told us about that, ma'am," he cut her off. Then pointed to the drawing of her suspect. "Is this a picture of Paul Hammetts?"

"No. At least, I don't think so. Like I said he's not my main suspect, it's—"

"Can I take it?"

"Well, okay," Mabel replied as he was already unpinning it.

"That's it for me."

Detective Tomlinson jumped in and said to Mabel, "We'll have more questions I'm sure, so make sure you are available. And nothing of what we shared with you today should be mentioned to any media so please refrain from talking to them again." Mabel felt completely misunderstood. "And stay away from the families. Don't mention anything we said to them because the last thing we need is a leak about the details of the case. Clear?"

Mabel nodded, flushed, and annoyed.

Detective Smith walked out. But Detective Tomlinson stayed and asked, "Any mention from the families about the girls wearing lots of makeup, wigs, or nail polish at home?"

Mabel shook her head. "I read about that."

"Don't mention that to anyone. The media loves details like that. And I can't stress enough: *Do not talk to the press!*" Detective Tomlinson glanced back at the wall, shaking her head. "And whatever you think you're doing here, drop it. That's our job."

Mabel sighed, and then nodded, deflated.

They both gave her their cards by the entrance and then left to get into their car, talking about Mabel like she wasn't even there. As Detective Smith got into the passenger seat, he carelessly tossed her folded-up notes and photos in the back seat before they drove off.

Mabel stood there for a long moment, feeling worthless and ashamed. Then she headed back defeated to the diner to finish her shift. As soon as she walked in, Molly grabbed her arm and whispered. "See that couple at the counter? They read your name in the paper and want to meet you."

Mabel's mood sunk even further. She whispered back, "Do you mind taking my shift?" Molly nodded. "And please tell them I'm not available. I don't want to talk to anyone about this."

Then Mabel fled home with her arms crossed, head down, feeling like a criminal.

CHAPTER 25

Saturday, November 28, 1987

Two weeks later, Mabel was sitting discretely at the back of a packed Tacoma funeral home, listening to the heartfelt tributes to Sandra Hoffman. Patty was sitting in front, looking gaunt and frail, wearing an ill-fitting black outfit that looked like it had been hastily thrown together. There was no mention of Sandra's father, nor did he appear to be present.

After the service, a long line of people formed to offer their condolences to Patty. She seemed surprised yet touched by the number of people attending.

When it was Mabel's turn, Patty recoiled upon seeing her.

"I am so sorry for your loss," Mabel offered.

"I thought I could trust you," Patty lashed out. "I read about my daughter's death in the papers! Why didn't you tell me instead of those journalists?"

"I didn't know," Mabel cried out. "I heard the same time as you."

"They shamed my daughter! Talking about how she was murdered like that."

"I am so sorry," Mabel repeated. "I wish I could have changed things."

"*You* told me you would find the murderer, but have you? Police tell me they have suspects, but no one is in jail. Everyone is lying to me, including you. And you're a mother too. You can go home to your kids. Your sons. But I have nothing. An empty house."

Another woman stepped in to give Mabel a scathing look. "I think you've done enough."

Mabel wanted to say more but seeing Patty so distraught, she said only, "I'm so sorry." Then Mabel drew away, saddened.

As she was leaving, a college-age woman pulled Mabel aside. It took a moment for Mabel to realize it was Kelly — the friend of Sandra she had talked to in Patty's home.

"Have they found the killer yet?"

"I don't know," Mabel replied, hurt. "The police are looking into suspects. I gave them all my notes and everything."

"Then what have *you* found out?"

"The police told me to stay away!"

Kelly gripped Mabel's arm tightly, hurting her, but Mabel didn't pull her arm away.

"You must find out who did this! I don't know what kind of sick person does this, but you need to find him. Put him away. Promise me."

"But I—"

"Promise!"

Mabel swallowed and then nodded. "I promise you."

Kelly searched Mabel's eyes for the truth, released her and then left to tend to Patty.

Mabel rubbed her arm to numb the pain, but she felt the imprint of Kelly's desperate grip all the way home.

CHAPTER 26

An hour later, back in her home office, the blank spaces on Mabel's corkboard felt like a betrayal. The detectives who had taken her notes and photos were looking for pedophiles across the region, but Samuel Ketch was not one of them.

She unpinned John Ford's business card from her wall and dialed his number.

"It's Mabel," she said after he picked up.

"How's your case?"

"Terrible, frankly. Two bodies were found out near Leavenworth."

"Oh, that's interesting."

His usual enthusiasm threw her for a second, but she kept on. "Well, uh, the *Seattle Times* is calling the

Dollhouse Killer case. Because the killer dressed them up in makeup and wigs."

"The press do like their catchy names."

"One of the Leavenworth girls was Sandra Hoffman, who'd I been trying to find. The poor dear was only bones, but a second victim, who I didn't know about, had been alive weeks ago. And when the detectives came to talk to me, they told me they're only looking for pedophiles in the region."

"Chasing down local pedophiles is not a bad thing. But you don't sound convinced."

"I met one of the men they're looking into — a Paul Hammetts. Actually, he came by my diner, and I called the sheriff to check him out. I caught him staring at two young girls. He fit my suspect description and all, but there's someone else too. I told the detectives this, but they didn't want to hear it. My suspect was supposed to have started Larson's house of horrors, and I can't imagine a worse person than that. And since you had mentioned these killers go back to the crime scene, I had the woods searched around here but found nothing."

"Okay, but keep in mind that it's the sentimental value to the abduction or murder that's important," Ford replied. "It's possible your suspect even visited Leavenworth now that it's been in the news. I often encourage police to watch out for gawkers who visit crime scenes because one might be the killer. They're intelligent, thoughtful, and meticulous. But they do make mistakes, and they may be drawn back to these sites based on their sexual or control fantasies. You say these girls had makeup on their face and nails? They obviously didn't wear this type of makeup at home?"

"No," Mabel said. "It was pretty garish, I read."

"That fact makes this even more interesting. The killer's treating girls like dolls, so the media isn't too far off with their name. And if he's infantilizing or over-sexualizing these girls, that might be what turns him on or makes him kill. You said during our last conversation that he had a controlling mother? Why do you suspect that?"

"I met her. But she has the Alzheimer's, so I don't know if what she's saying is the disease or really what she means."

"Did she say anything about Samuel — her son?"

"Well, she both praised him and then called him a…" She cleared her throat, uncomfortable and not wanting to say it. "Excuse me, a mean word. And she hates her husband who had passed."

John chuckled. "That helps your profile, at least. Mental instability and abuse in the home fits the pattern. Did she mention anything about the son playing with dolls?"

Mabel deflated. "I didn't ask. But he visits her twice a week and takes care of her, brushes her hair, and does things like that."

"Ask her then. Find out if she remembers anything about that. Then find out if he had an alibi. Are the dates of deaths known?"

"It hasn't been released yet."

"Okay, so an alibi won't help. But see if the mother can remember anything about Leavenworth. What's around there? Is that near you?"

"If people know Leavenworth, they know Blue River."

"You're on the right track then. Talk to your suspect. But remember, don't focus everything on him — the detectives might be right on this Paul Hammetts. Profiles by nature will fit many people and that's why it's a profile. Chasing down the known pedophiles in the region is a good strategy. But I agree with you; it can't be the only tactic. Has your suspect made any overtures to the press, yet?"

"No. I mean … not that I am aware of."

"Okay, watch out for that." He paused. "So, you think there're fifteen more?"

"Yes."

"And those detectives weren't interested in that?"

"Not that I can tell."

John huffed. "Okay, I'll see if those detectives made a support request to my unit. I'm interested in this case based on what you told me. There could be several body drop-off sites. Leavenworth may be the first, but there could be others or soon to be others. My killers travel across regions to cover their tracks. Keep doing what you're doing and find out which places your suspect or suspects have visited." John paused and said something offline before he came back on. "Okay, I got to go. If your detectives haven't made a request yet,

I can't officially jump in. But if you find more bodies, call me. Like I said, this is interesting."

"Well, I'm glad you think so because the two detectives told me to stop. And I almost did."

"Don't listen to them."

Mabel looked at the empty spaces on her wallboard where the detectives had taken her photos and notes. "I promise you, I won't make that mistake again."

CHAPTER 27

Tuesday, December 1, 1987

Mabel walked her kids to the school bus and watched it pull away as the sun crested the forested ridge, bathing her motel and diner in morning light. Her place opened later than usual today due to the slowdown in customers, and only Kevin and Molly were in the kitchen. Mabel unlocked the main door and started getting the dining area organized.

Ed, the deliveryman, came in to drop off a stack of newspapers on the counter. He greeted Mabel cheerily and then chatted up Molly. And Mabel wondered if those two would ever go out. Both widowers with kids away in college, they would be a good match. Once Ed left, Molly hummed a cheerful tune while cutting open the twine of the newspaper bundle, so Mabel teased, "Looks like you and Ed are getting along nicely."

"Oh, you," Molly said, with a giggle. "He's nice and—"

Molly gasped in horror and dropped the stack.

"Are you okay?" Mabel rushed over.

Molly shook her head, pointing at it.

Mabel swept up the top paper, and on its front page, the blaring headline "Dollhouse Killer Caught!" was accompanied by a picture of the police arresting Paul Hammetts.

"It *was* him!" Molly cried, shaking. "He was here!"

Mabel read on. A sex offender for the past ten years, Mr. Hammetts, a Métis from Canada, divorced with two kids, had a previous conviction for propositioning twelve-year-old girls in Seattle.

"Oh my God, Mabel! That's so scary. To think he might have gone after the Wilson girls too! But you did it! You called it in to Dan and helped police find the killer!" She came over to hug Mabel, then stopped short. "Aren't you happy?"

"I am, dear. But it's just…" Mabel paused, thinking it through. Then she shook it off, pulled Molly in for a hug, and got the chills as it slowly sank in that the girls' killer was in jail.

* * *

With her emotions barely in check, Mabel quickly took her leave from the diner and went to find Bill and tell him the good news. But by the time she saw him in the kitchen at home, her emotions burst out, startling him, as she rushed into his arms. "Oh Bill," she cried. "They found the killer!"

He wrapped his big arms around her, and his warmth and strength enveloped her as she cried for several minutes. He held her tight without saying anything, which was exactly what she needed. When she finally eased back, his big hands wiped the tears off her cheeks, and she smiled, embarrassed. "I'm such a waterworks," she said, reaching back to get a tissue to finish drying her eyes.

"Who did it?"

Mabel told him who, and Bill was shocked, shaking his head. "To think that SOB was a customer."

Mabel shivered, staying silent.

"And the Wilson sisters. My God! That's disgusting! It's a good thing Molly pointed him out and you called it in, or otherwise…" He let the sentence hang and Mabel felt her gut twist. Then he added, "Well, at least I'll get my office back now."

She pushed him. "Oh you!"

He laughed. Then brought her back in close. "You keep moving my stuff. What am I supposed to do?"

She pressed her hands against his chest in protest for his trying to make light of this, but she didn't move away either. "What am I going to do with you?"

"We'll think of something," he said and then turned around to do something even more surprising. He started doing the dishes.

"Oh my God," she said. "Are you doing the dishes?"

"Oh come on now! I'm not that bad!" He paused. "Well … sometimes." He smiled and then told her. "Go take a load off in the den. I'll bring you a coffee."

She liked the sound of that, kissed his neck, and then hugged his chest from behind, and he held her hand for a moment before she left. In the den, she stared out the window, barely noticing the picturesque mountain view as she thought about the girls.

The ringing of the phone jolted her back to the present.

"Mabel's Diner and—" she stopped herself. Then simply said, "Mabel speaking."

"Mabel!" sounded the friendly voice of Lavi Arronson, the public defender who had gotten Mabel into the PI business to begin with.

"Lavi! So nice to hear from you. I haven't talked to you in a while."

"I've been busy."

"And how's your mother."

"Oh, good, good. Feeling a little better these days. But it's a struggle, as you know. She says hi, by the way. She sure appreciated the baking you dropped off yesterday."

"Always a pleasure with her. And where were you? She said you were busy."

"I was and I am. And I'm sorry I missed your visit, but I was handed a priority case." Lavi cleared his throat. "Which is, um, why I need to talk to you. This one's going to be tough. Did you read the paper today?"

"Just the front page. Did you see? They caught my killer," she replied with a laugh, expecting him to react too. But he went dead silent, so she prompted, "Aren't you going to say something?"

"That's it."

"What's it?"

"That's my case."

Mabel took a moment before she figured out what he meant. "You're joking! You're representing Paul Hammetts? Oh, dear Lord, Lavi. That man harms children."

"I need the best. I need you."

She scoffed. "Come on! I have no interest in helping someone like that."

"Think of the law."

"Think of their mothers, Lavi. The police must think he did it. Why else would they bring him in?"

"All circumstantial."

"Then why would they arrest him on it?"

"You remember Winston, right?"

"That case was different. Winston was innocent."

"So is Paul."

"He hurts children!"

"Yes, okay, he's guilty of that. But not murder. He's been punished for those crimes and has gone through years of therapy. I talked to his psychologist yesterday. It's not in his nature to kill."

"I'm not helping a man that hurts children! I'm the one who caught him staring at two girls in my diner and called it in to Dan in the first place! That's why the police picked him up."

"He has an explanation for that."

"I can imagine. But I'm not helping that man."

"Then what about the mothers?"

"Paul Hammetts' mother has to deal with the Lord's grace, not me."

"I meant the mothers of your missing girls."

Mabel sat up, too upset to speak but getting ready to give Lavi a piece of her mind.

Lavi pressed on. "What if the killer is still out there? What if Paul isn't the killer? And the real killer hurts more girls while he is in jail, falsely accused. This is bigger than his innocence. This is justice, Mabel. This is stopping the real killer. Not picking a scapegoat that fits the bill simply because he's done bad things. We can't let the police get distracted by him. I want the real killer in jail just as much as you. Paul admitted guilt to his past crimes and has been punished. He says he's innocent with this and I believe him. I know you have that gift of yours. Use it here."

Mabel scoffed, struggling mightily until she thought of Patty and Kelly and her promise to keep going. With her fingertips squeezing the bridge of her nose, she said, "Ughh! I *could* meet him, I guess."

"You're the best. When do you want to come?"

"I didn't say I would do it!" Mabel growled. "Ugh! How fast can we get this over with?"

"I can meet you at the King County Jail — same place you met Kyle — in two hours."

Mabel fumed as she considered it. Then, she said petulantly, "Okay."

"See you there." Lavi hung up and the dial tone droned.

Mabel slammed down the receiver.

CHAPTER 28

Lavi stood beside Mabel as the guard explained the rules, but Mabel — steaming mad and familiar with the drill anyway — was only half-listening. While driving up, she had changed her mind and intended to tell Lavi she wouldn't go through with it, but he had deliberately waited inside the jail's second holding area, forcing her to go through the elaborate and lengthy security checks. And once she had made it this far, it didn't make sense to turn around, which was why Lavi was still smiling, and she was irate.

The guard finished his spiel and then opened the gate, letting them in.

Lavi had requested a private room used for lawyer-client discussions. As a defense lawyer, Lavi was friendly with the guards and sent them little gifts for the holidays. Not bribes, he made it clear to Mabel. Everything was by the book, but it got him special treatment, nonetheless.

The guard opened the second door, and Mabel hesitated, still annoyed until Lavi touched her arm. Since he disliked physical contact of any kind and that gesture was so unlike him, it prompted her to walk in.

Paul Hammetts sat shackled behind a white metal table on which Lavi set his briefcase. Lavi gestured for her to sit as well. With Paul's mustache and round face, he looked just like her suspect drawing.

Mabel's glare withered him, and he seemed to shrink into his orange prison jumpsuit. Without the ball cap to shade his mousy features, his dark eyes no longer seemed so menacing. At least the skinheads, Mabel thought, openly proclaimed their evil with their tattoos, biker dress, and shaved heads. This man would blend into a crowd as he hunted children, just like John Ford had said.

Lavi introduced him to Mabel and then prompted Paul to tell his story. Instead, Paul looked directly at her and asked, "You think I'm a monster, don't you?"

Mabel huffed and turned away, shaking her head, furious she had to sit through this.

"I've admitted to my problems, I'm in counseling."

"Counseling? I saw you looking at those girls in my diner. It isn't working."

"I can't help it. It's who I am."

"You harm children!"

"I haven't harmed anyone!" Paul protested. "Honest! I haven't touched a girl since my first arrest. And yes, the ... the urges are still there. I can't help it. But the counseling is ... it's why I don't act on them. That's the difference now." He stopped to calm himself. "I didn't kill anyone. I'm not a killer."

Mabel locked eyes with him to root out the evil she had seen before and, to her surprise, she also saw the truth.

She shifted in her seat and looked away, not knowing what to say. She was still disgusted with him, but at least her anger had evaporated, and she could breathe again. She began to ask him some questions.

"Why were you at my diner?"

He sighed. "I was at home and I ... I just couldn't handle it anymore. I had to get out. Drive. Like my counselor says — change the environment. I drove for hours to escape my urges, but I couldn't do it. I saw your diner and stopped because I was thirsty. And when I saw those girls..." He exhaled a long, slow breath. "My thoughts returned. And I, uh, I tried journaling like my therapist says. It helped." He looked away and then down. "Sort of."

"Would you have harmed them?"

"No! Maybe, I don't know. I hope not."

"Are you getting counseling here?" He nodded. "You're not cured, you know." He nodded again, and she calmed some more. Then she asked, "Did you do it? Did you kill those girls found in the woods by Leavenworth?"

"No," he said, firmly holding her gaze.

Lavi turned to Mabel and she cleared her throat to speak, but no words came out. But Lavi waited silently, and after a long moment, Mabel gave him the slightest nod.

He tried but failed to hide a smile as he opened his briefcase on the table.

Mabel resumed her questioning. "Sandra Hoffman and Tracy Richards were sixteen, just like those girls at my diner."

"I thought the girls were younger, about twelve. They were pretty."

"Don't you dare talk about them like that!"

Paul flinched and looked down again.

Mabel breathed through her surging anger, trying to think rationally. "What is your alibi?"

Lavi cut in. "He doesn't have one."

Mabel ignored Lavi and waited for Paul to answer.

"I live alone."

"You told the sheriff you had a fight with your wife."

"I lied."

"Why?"

Paul shrugged. "I figured he wouldn't arrest me if he thought I was still married."

Mabel allowed him that and nodded slowly. "What about your kids?"

Paul deflated and rubbed his neck. "After my first arrest, she divorced me and took them. Most of my community back in Canada — I'm Métis — disowned me. No one wants anything to do with me. I work at a business supply store in Tacoma. I stock shelves. I stay home, read books, watch television, go to therapy. The night I was at your diner, my therapist was on vacation. That's why I went for a drive. Because when I don't work, I'm home. I'm not allowed to go anywhere near schools or where kids go, so I don't go anywhere. I got nothing and I don't have much money saved. Which is why" — he waved absently at Lavi — "I got him."

"You are very lucky to have him!"

Paul flinched, looking down again.

Mabel released her glare from Paul and turned to Lavi. "So? What's next?"

"That's up to you."

"Well," she said, thinking it through. "We need to find out who really did this."

Lavi leaned in closer to her and whispered, "Are you going to talk to your suspect?"

Mabel shook her head and whispered back: "His mother."

CHAPTER 29

Thursday, December 3, 1987

B ack at the Englewood Retirement Facility, Mabel had asked the receptionist if she could visit Angelica when the bearded male nurse standing behind said, "I'll take you."

As he led Mabel down the corridor, he asked, "Are you family of Ms. Kerns?"

"No. I'm just here on a visit."

"So…" He drew out the word. "You know what to expect, right?"

"I've been here before."

"Okay, good. She can be quite a handful, to put it mildly. Even quite abusive."

"I'm aware she has the Alzheimer's."

"It's not just that. Doc thinks she has an undiagnosed psychiatric disorder and her added cognitive issues are only making it worse. I feel sorry for her son. He seems to get the brunt of it."

"Samuel?"

He nodded. "She shouts some pretty horrible things when he's here — we can hear her down the hall — and it disturbs a lot of our other visitors and guests, so we like to warn people about Ms. Kerns. But if she tries to leave the room, tell us. She's been known to escape the property — even with all our checks. If you have any issues, come to the front desk."

"Thank you. I will."

"Well, here's her room. Good luck," he said and then continued down the hall.

Angelica's bed was partially upright, and she was staring at the far wall, hair askew and face bare of makeup.

"Hello Ms. Kerns? Do you mind if I come in? It's me, Mabel."

Angelica blinked several times before her cataract-clouded eyes zeroed in on Mabel. A thin, slow smile started forming; then it melted into a scowl. "Took you long enough to get here."

"Oh, I came unannounced. Sorry, I should have called ahead—"

"I don't have my makeup on! Get here faster next time, you son-of-a-bitch!"

Mabel pressed her palm to her heart, aware Angelica might be talking about her son. "I-It's me, Mabel. I'm an investigator."

Angelica squinted, then reached for her glasses and put them on. Her eyes became as big as saucers. Then she beamed and in the sweetest voice said, "Oh, I remember you from last time, dear. You were asking me about my sweet little boy. Come in and sit."

Mabel suppressed a shudder and sat down. "I do have more questions about your son Ton—" she caught herself in time. "Samuel. When he was young."

Angelica cackled. "He's still young, dear. My Sammie's in first grade."

Mabel paused, recognizing where Angelica was in her timeline, and went with it. "Does he play well with the girls in his class?"

Angelica sighed. "Boys will be boys."

"No. I mean, does he play with dolls and such?"

Angelica's face slowly twisted into a mask of rage as she yelled at the door. "How dare you go into my things! Look how you ruined them! You're a no-good father's boy, stop touching my things!" Mabel shifted, disconcerted. The hall was empty, as before. Then Angelica blinked and smiled. "Why, it's so nice to have visitors."

Mabel breathed out her unease, ignoring her outburst. "What things? What made you mad? Was he wearing something of yours?"

"My Samuel would never do such things. Whatever made you say that?"

"When he was young, I mean."

"My Samuel helps me with my makeup and my hair," she said, posing like a model. But when she touched her hair to shake it, she frowned and her voice became harsh again. "That bastard was supposed to do my hair today. He embarrasses me. Always embarrasses me. I raised him to be a man. But he's not a man." She glared at the door with such malice in her eyes. "He's a freak, like his father! They're just the same."

Mabel leaned forward, eager to hear more. "What do you mean?"

A man's voice spoke from the door. "What are you doing here?"

Mabel started. "Oh, my God! You scared me half to—"

She gasped in shock.

Samuel Ketch walked in the room and placed his hat on the dresser. "What are you doing here with my mother?"

"Well, I…"

Angelica cut in. "She's asking me questions, dear. About you."

His voice was raw. "What questions?"

"Don't you use that tone with me!" Angelica said and put her hand on Mabel's arm to pull her in close, surprisingly strong. "She's keeping me company. Unlike you. You're always late."

"I'm always on time, mother." Then he turned to Mabel. "You should leave."

Mabel got up. "I'm sorry for intruding. But I have some questions for you too."

He ignored her by striding into the hall, and shouted, "Nurse!"

The bearded nurse walked up. "Yes?"

"This woman is trespassing."

"Her? I don't understand," the nurse said. "She said she was a family friend."

"No. She's an investigator hassling my mother. She isn't family. She's an intruder."

The male nurse threw Mabel a sharp, disappointed look. "You didn't tell me that."

"Well, I—"

Samuel cut Mabel off. "I want this woman out of here. I don't want her seeing my mother again."

The male nurse said to Mabel, "You need to leave, or I'll call security."

"I'm filing a complaint," Samuel growled to the nurse. "And if she ever shows up here again, I'm going to pull my mother out of this center."

The male nurse gestured for Mabel to leave. "Ma'am, please."

Mabel turned to Samuel, "Can I talk to you outside?"

"No."

"I have questions for you about the murdered girls near Leavenworth."

The male nurse spoke louder, gesturing for her to move back. "Ma'am! This way."

Mabel spoke over his shoulder to Samuel. "You need to talk to me."

Samuel turned to the nurse. "I won't stand for this."

"Now," the nurse demanded of Mabel. "Or I'm calling security."

"You don't have to do that." Mabel gave in. "I'm going." Then she turned to Samuel, "You're going to have to answer my questions sometime."

He sneered with disdain. "That's fine, Mabel. I know where you live."

Mabel froze.

Then as Samuel went back into the room, she asked the nurse, "Did he just threaten me?"

"Keep moving, ma'am. I shouldn't have let you in."

"I'm sorry. I didn't mean to get you in trouble. But he just—"

"Please leave," the nurse said, guiding her to the main door. "Now!"

Mabel was led away, catching the stares of everyone in the hall. Then the nurse shut the main doors and stood guard.

As Mabel slowly turned and walked to her car, she realized what a mess she had made. She looked back at the center one last time and her eyes widened.

Samuel was staring at her from Angelica's room.

Then he swept the curtains shut.

CHAPTER 30

Friday, December 4, 1987

Kerry shouted into the phone's receiver, causing Mabel to nearly fall off her office chair. "Are you still there? Oh, God! I am so, so sorry. I guess Katie yelled into the bathroom that you were on the line, but I couldn't hear her over Susan's blow dryer. It wasn't until I finished my makeup and was vegging out in the common room waiting for your call when Katie asked, 'How is your Aunt?' and I said, 'I haven't talked to her yet!' and that's when she told me you were still on and well, that's why I'm late! Sorry-y-y!"

Mabel laughed, having already reset herself on the chair and caught up to the conversation. "All good. You just caught me thinking, is all."

"About the case?"

"Well ... yes."

"That's good. Because I got some news for you!" Kerry's sing song voice shifted to a more conspiratorial tone. "About the death of Mr. Ketch. And let me tell you, it seems fishy to me."

"What did you find?"

"It took me a while. I can tell you that. But I took your advice and asked the librarian for help. She was good, but still, it meant spending hours and hours going through old news reports and—"

Mabel cut in. "What about your studies?"

"Oh, I don't mind. This is more important and—"

"Kerry! Your studies are very important!"

Kerry sighed. "I know. It's just ... ugh, I can't sleep at night. Thinking of those girls. And what they must have been through." Her voice cracked. "I know what it's like."

Mabel touched her heart, deeply concerned, but all she could say was: "I'm so sorry."

After a long silence, Kerry sniffled before she blew her nose and said, "Not sleeping I guess is way better than the nightmares."

Mabel winced. "Is there someone else you can talk to about this?"

Kerry sighed. "I do ... but I don't. My friends ... they, uh, just don't understand. And boys? Well, they're just looking for a good time." Mabel frowned, taking a note of that last comment as Kerry went on. "And well, this helps. It does. It takes my mind off what I went through and makes it feel like it wasn't all in vain. I don't want to be a victim. I want some control back. This gives it to me."

Mabel pressed the phone tighter to her ear, wishing she could be there to hold Kerry just as tightly. She wanted to ask about what happened, but understood that Kerry didn't want that now, so Mabel reluctantly returned to the case. "What did you learn?"

Kerry cleared her throat and then added in a hushed voice. "Okay. Get this. I think it was murder."

"What?"

"I know, right? The papers didn't say it as such, but Mr. Ketch was an otherwise healthy older man, late fifties, who apparently up and died one day sitting at the kitchen table with his wife. The obit said that the coroner's report was inconclusive — so not a heart attack, right? And get this, Angelica didn't put the obit in the paper. His friends did. She didn't even have a funeral for him. So I got in touch with the local paper who gave me the contact of the man who wrote the obit, an old friend of Mr. Ketch. He said he never liked Angelica, thought she was too controlling, and he always wondered why there was no funeral because Mr. Ketch was well-liked and lots of people wanted a chance to pay their respects. It got a lot of people asking questions, and the man said, 'Angelica didn't like that.' So I guess she moved away with her son soon after and disappeared."

"So there was no follow-up? No police investigation?"

"None."

"Is there anything else I should know?"

"Um … I haven't found anything yet. But I'll keep digging."

Mabel regretted now more than ever that the retirement home banned her from speaking with Angelica as it left her with few options. But she didn't want Kerry to be so involved so she changed the subject. "I take it you haven't read a Seattle paper this week?"

"No, why? I've been buried in all the old ones."

Mabel gave her an update on Paul Hammetts and her role with Lavi in trying to prove his innocence. When she finished, Kerry added, "Oh my God! I can't believe it! You're in the papers!"

Mabel huffed, as that wasn't what she wanted to focus on, but Kerry laughed in turn. "Don't worry, I'm teasing you, and I know how humble you are. And yes, I am going back to the library tonight to read those papers! My friends are loving the fact that you are such a badass PI!"

"Kerry!" Mabel pleaded, too embarrassed by it all.

Kerry laughed again. "Auntie, you are one of a kind."

Mabel sighed. "That's what Bill keeps saying."

"Well, he's right. And he's lucky to have you. So, how's it going with him?"

Mabel glossed over her concerns. "I think good. I hope so. It's nice having him around again. He's doing more around the house too, even cleaning!"

Kerry chuckled. "Well, times are a changing. A lot of girls here don't even know how to cook. And let me tell you, any boy I date better know how or learn fast. And he better clean too."

Mabel's eyes lit up. "Anyone worth talking about?"

Kerry stammered. "Oh … uh, I gotta bounce. Sorry. Susan needs to use the phone. Love you! Bye!"

Mabel didn't even have a chance to say bye back, and as she slowly hung up, she started to wonder what secrets Kerry was hiding too.

CHAPTER 31

Monday, December 7, 1987

Every bump in the night or house creak during the day sent her heart thudding as Samuel's last words echoed in her mind: "I know where you live." The latest creak outside on the porch had brought her to the den window. But nothing was there. Even with all of Larson's threats, she had never locked all her doors and windows before, but she was now. Bill tried to placate her fears and said, "Honey, you got a man in the house. He ain't going to bother you."

A screech of brakes and grinding tires on gravel announced the school bus had arrived. Her boys got off together, talking and laughing, and Mabel waved, happy to see them. Having Bill home had done wonders for them. They fought less and played more. She turned to open the front door when—

A piercing scream sent her rushing outside.

Hector was holding a terrified Fred, who was pointing at the porch and crying hysterically.

Mabel looked to where he was pointing and saw a porcelain doll, naked, arms splayed out, garish makeup on its face, its body splashed with blood.

Mabel edged past it with horror then shouted toward the motel. "Bill! Bill! Come quick!"

She swept her two boys inside, shielding Fred from the doll while Hector tried to look around her.

"Come on, Mom, what is it?"

"You watch your brother inside!"

"Ah, Mom, I want to see."

"Go on! Now. I'm going to talk to your father."

Bill ran up the porch steps but stopped short seeing the bloody doll. He picked it up and then used a finger to taste the liquid.

"Bill! Don't do that!"

He made a bitter face as he spit it out. "It's blood," he said. "What sick mind would do this?"

"I think I know who would," Mabel growled.

"Then I'm tossing it in the trash."

"No!" Mabel gripped his arm. "Evidence. Put it in the motel office for now, so the boys don't see it."

Bill left with it, as she herded the kids away from the den window and into the kitchen. They had a thousand questions, but she settled them inside with a bribe of ice cream and a promise to tell them later. When Bill came back in, he jerked his head signalling for her to join him in the hall. "It's in the motel office now," he whispered. "I called Dan too. He's coming over."

Mabel made to reply but then spied Hector peeking around the wall.

"Do you mind?" she asked, putting her hands on her hips.

"I want to stay! I'm old enough."

Bill stepped in. "He's right. He *is* old enough."

"What? No!" Mabel protested. "You get back in the kitchen."

"Ahhh, Mom!"

"Git."

Hector sulked, dragging his feet, until Mabel swatted his bum with a dishcloth and he ran back.

Bill started in. "It's about time he does more. He's twelve, for god's sakes. I can't always be—"

"Not now, Bill." Mabel's tone was sharp as she cut him off. "Dan just pulled up," she added and then led the way to his cruiser outside.

"Morning Mabel, Bill," Dan said, tipping his sheriff's hat. "Now, what's all this craziness?"

Bill led them to the motel office, where he pulled out the doll from where he'd hidden it under the desk. "It's blood."

Dan dabbed his finger to taste it, disgusting Mabel, but since Bill seemed none the worse for it either, she said nothing.

Dan spit it out. "Bill's right. But what does this mean? I can't see any of Larson's boys playing with dolls and such. They'd just come in and crack heads."

Mabel finally voiced her suspicion. "I visited Angelica — my suspect's mother — four days ago. That's when Samuel Ketch threatened me."

"What?" Dan exclaimed. "Why?"

"Because he's a killer," Mabel declared, arms crossed. Then conceded. "Well ... maybe."

"You mean the Dollhouse Killer? But they caught the guy."

Mabel shook her head. "I interviewed Paul Hammetts in jail. He didn't do it, Dan."

Dan rubbed his face. "Oh jeez. You helping him now? I thought he harmed kids."

"Well ... it's a long story. But it's not him. I looked into his eyes and he's no killer. But if he isn't, then the killer or killers are still out there. That's why I visited Angelica." She pointed at the doll. "And that's his message back."

Dan took off his hat to rub his hair. "Not again," he said finally, looking at her. "This investigative stuff of yours is dangerous."

Mabel breathed out, glancing at Bill, and then looked down at her shoes.

"I guess there's no use trying to change your mind, though," Dan said to her. Mabel shook her head, and then looked up. "That's what I thought." Dan sighed. "I'll take this doll then as evidence and ask around if anyone saw anything, maybe your customers or staff and such."

Mabel touched his arm, appreciative. "I'm sorry. I didn't think this would come back to us. I thought we were done with this too."

Dan slicked his hair back to put on his sheriff's hat as he said, "Aw shoot, Mabel. If you hadn't meddled in the first place, Larson and his boys would still be running this place. I know a lotta folks here don't see it, but I do."

"Well," Mabel said, pausing a moment until she got their attention. "You both might like to hear this, but I don't think I want to be doing this investigating no more."

Bill beamed as Dan said, "That's the first good news I've heard all day!"

"I didn't say I was stopping this minute!" Mabel added quickly. But their enthusiasm didn't wane, so she playfully scolded them, "Oh, get on with both of ya!"

Dan laughed before he grabbed the doll and shooed them both outside. "You two go on home and relax. I got this one. Let me bag it, then show it around and get some answers back to you, pronto."

"Thanks Dan," Mabel said, thankful he was taking it seriously. "And make sure you tell the state detectives too that I think it's Samuel Ketch. They didn't believe me last time and this should change their minds if anything will."

CHAPTER 32

Tuesday, December 8, 1987

Mabel stood by her den window to watch for the afternoon school bus, and she was surprised to see Dan getting out of his cruiser and then Bill crossing the gravel lot to talk to him. Hoping for news, Mabel rushed out too. As she met them by the cruiser, Bill craned his neck to peer into Dan's occupied back seat. "Who you got in there?"

"Hooligans."

Mabel pressed her hands to her heart.

"Not your boys," Dan said quickly, reading her perfectly. "But I got two miscreants here who need to tell ya something." He opened his cruiser's back door and growled, "Git out and do what I told ya."

Jacob and Isaiah Hudgens, two well-known bullies that had physically sprouted up and out in the last year, crawled out, embarrassed. Both were now taller than Mabel.

Dan cuffed Jacob in the back of the head. "Go on. Tell her what you told me." Jacob looked down at the ground and said nothing until Dan growled, "Go on!"

Jacob rubbed his arm for comfort as he said in a low voice, "My brother and I thought it would be funny." Mabel looked confused at Bill, so Dan poked Jacob's shoulder to prompt him.

Jacob pointed at the porch, speaking up now. "We left it there."

Dan commanded, "The whole story now."

Jacob kept shifting his feet as he explained, "We thought it would be funny. You were in the paper and all, and my dad wasn't too happy about that. Seeing what you done to the town and all. So, we took our sister's doll and my mom's makeup, and Isaiah here added the chicken blood from a fresh kill in the yard."

Mabel gasped, turning to the brother. "Is this true?"

Isaiah replied, downcast, "Yes, ma'am."

"So, you two did this?"

They both nodded.

Mabel almost laughed from relief, and Bill suppressed a smile too. Both had been so worried that it was a threat from a killer, they hadn't even considered it was simply two local kids playing a prank. But Dan wasn't finished with them. "You ain't done yet! Tell her!"

They nodded and both said, almost at the same time, "We're sorry ma'am. We shouldn'a done it."

Dan growled again. "And you're going to do more than just apologize, right?"

"Yes'em," Jacob said. "Whatever you need, ma'am. We're here to work it off."

Mabel and Bill looked at each other. Bill shrugged, and said, "I got nothing. I just finished the renovations."

Mabel looked around, thinking about it. "Well, my cook, Kevin, has about a day's worth of dishes backed up. He'd sure appreciate some washing help."

Dan slightly shook his head like that wasn't enough, even as the kids groaned.

"And..." Mabel added, enjoying this. "The stockroom needs to be taken down and cleaned and the grease traps above the stove need scrubbing."

Both Jacob and Isaiah protested loudly. "What?"

Dan smiled as took off his hat. "That's more like it." Then he growled at the kids, "Go on. Git. You got your orders. And you best be respectful in there and not break one dish or I'll haul you back to your mom and she'll hide you herself."

Jacob and Isaiah practically ran to the diner.

Mabel laughed and turned to Dan. "How did you know?"

"Kevin saw these two loitering around. And I knew these kids don't come here to play — your son not being friendly with them and all, and rightly so, for what they done to him last year. So, I put the twos and twos together and went to the school to have a talk with them." He slapped his hat against his leg and chuckled. "They put up some resistance, I tells ya. Tried to lie to me at first, but it's darn easy to tell when kids are fibbing. So I separated 'em and got 'em to turn on each other pretty quick. I called their ma about what I was planning to do here and she agreed. And she said once you're done with them, she's going to give them a few licks too."

Mabel laughed with him. "You know Dan. That doll scared me pretty good. But it's good to see it was pretty innocent, after all."

"That's good to hear. So, are you going to stop all this investigating and let me do my job from now on?" Dan asked, half-serious, and then glanced at Bill for support.

Bill raised his palms in the air. "I ain't sayin' anything. I'm just the hired hand."

"Ugh!" Mabel scolded Bill. "You git! Go put your tools away!"

"Yes, ma'am," Bill said contritely and then winked at Dan with a chuckle.

Dan waited till Bill left before he turned serious. "I almost had a heart attack thinking we were back to the troubles of last year. But Larson ain't around no more, thanks to you, and his men are mostly done and gone. But if anything brews up again, you know where to find me. I'm on it."

"Thanks, Dan." She touched his arm appreciatively. Then she guided him back to his cruiser, and asked, "Are we still on for Saturday?"

Dan made a face like he wasn't looking forward to it. "Speaking of getting someone killed. My ma ain't going to like it."

"Dan. It's time she knows. About you and Kennie. You two are happy together."

"You don't know my ma."

"I'll be there to support you. It'll be fine."

"I don't know," Dan said, exhaling slowly. "I think I'd rather face Larson again."

Mabel laughed.

Dan didn't.

CHAPTER 33

Wednesday, December 9, 1987

An owl hooted from the woods outside Mabel's bedroom window. The night's breeze picked up, rustling the dead leaves outside. She snuggled deeper under the warm sheets, and Bill lightly caressed her back.

He asked, "Babe?"

"Hmmm?"

"I need to talk to you about something." His hand stopped moving.

Mabel glanced back and, upon seeing his pained expression, immediately propped herself up with her elbow. "What is it?"

Bill wouldn't look at her.

"What is it?" she asked again, concerned

"I've, um…" He cleared his throat roughly. "Been drinking again."

Her breathing stopped.

Her world crumbled.

Then she sat upright, ready to fight, to yell, to scream.

But he looked so defeated, her heart softened. But this … this!

She fought with her conflicting emotions until tears started streaming down both their faces, and so she touched his hand to connect, not knowing what to think. The last time she'd confronted him about his drinking, he had denied it. Tonight, he'd come clean about his relapse, and she didn't know what to say.

He rubbed his tear-stained cheeks with his forearm and growled. "I hate fucking up like this."

"Have you tried to stop?"

Bill sucked in his breath. "I've tried. Trust me, I've tried. It started just after the trade show. I was so furious with Walter, for what he done. I was angry. I didn't know what to think. I found a beer in a motel room" — Mabel cursed herself for not getting rid of it in time — "and I drank it without thinking. I almost didn't even taste it. Then I crumpled it up and threw it away, and I vowed I wouldn't do it again. But then, a few days later I got a craving. I thought, just one. That's it. Then I'd be done. But it wasn't. The kids…" Bill stopped and glanced at Mabel. "They almost caught me once. I'm sorry. I hid it. I think Hector might have suspected, but I don't know. I don't know what to do Mabel. I'm sorry."

Mabel touched Bill's hand again and he gripped hers so tightly it hurt, but she didn't pull away. Instead, she put her other hand on his cheek and said, "We can get through this."

Bill looked down, crying, but she turned his face gently up so he could look into her eyes.

"We *can* get through this," she repeated.

"I'm sorry," he said. Then he hung his head again. "I thought I was better."

Mabel pulled him to her chest, feeling overwhelmed, but she comforted him without talking until his breathing finally slowed, and he fell asleep. Then she gently eased out from under him to sit on the edge of the bed. By then her anger had lessoned, but an intense sadness remained, and she watched the full moon track higher and higher until it finally pierced a bank of dark clouds, lost to view.

* * *

She awoke to a cold, empty bed but the sound of plates and cups being set on the kitchen table told her where Bill was. She put on her housecoat and went downstairs to talk.

He wouldn't look at her, so she hugged him, and he finally responded by kissing her hair.

"Bill, I..." She started but then stopped as the boys came barreling down for breakfast. And considering the circumstances, it was a surprisingly good meal together, though Bill's laughs were forced, and he had trouble hiding his pain. Fortunately, the boys didn't notice, and he helped them get dressed for school.

When Fred and Hector ran out to the bus, Bill followed them out to wave, and then stared at the empty road long after the bus had left. When he came back in, he said, defeated, "I got the last bit of cleanup to do in the motel. Then it's done."

Mabel didn't care about that. But her anger had come back, and she didn't want to talk about it now in case she said too much.

She ended up scrubbing the kitchen floors even though they'd just been cleaned. Mabel was mad at herself for not seeing that beer when she had first cleaned the rooms. Mad at Walter Hudson and that mine for causing all this in the first place. Mad at Bill for giving in to temptation. She finished up a half-hour later and was still angry, and so carried on, cleaning the entire house. By 2 PM, she was finally exhausted, and ready to talk.

Bill had just returned, but he had gone straight upstairs, so she went up to him. But when she caught him packing his travel duffel bag, she froze.

"What are you doing?"

Bill pulled more clothes from a drawer and tossed them on the bed. "A trade show is on in Minneapolis. I wasn't thinking of going, but I think maybe I should now."

"Aren't you going to say bye to the kids?"

Bill shook his head. "Best to head off now."

"When are you coming back?"

"It's a week-long one and I expect to sell out all my stock. And even if I don't, I'll be heading off to prospect for at least a few weeks, maybe a month, I'm thinking."

"A month!"

"Maybe more."

"Why?"

Bill stopped packing and held his clothes like he would tear them apart. "I had another drink today, Mabel. An hour ago. Even after all that talk last night, I can't stop myself."

Mabel stepped forward to turn him towards her. "We can do this together."

His voice was raw as he said, "We tried that last time. I need to get better. This is the only way I know how."

"But I can help you!"

Bill turned back to roughly packing his clothes. "I would have left days ago, but I thought you were in danger, so I stayed. But those Hudgens brats were just messing with us. Now, I am the most dangerous thing for you and the boys. I can't trust myself. I keep catching myself from getting mad at them. At you. It's taking everything I have to…" He sighed. "I want to get better for you. For our family."

"Then stay!"

Bill shook his head.

Mabel pushed his chest to knock it out of him, and shouted, "This is going to hurt those boys real bad!"

"I'll be back. I just … need more time."

She shouted, starting to cry, "I didn't want you coming in and out of their lives! It's too disruptive!"

He zipped up his duffel bag and slung it over his shoulder. He paused at the door, hung his head, and then came back to Mabel. With one hand, he pulled her in tight though she fought him.

Then he kissed her hard and their tears mixed on their cheeks. When he finally released her, she didn't know what to think. She wanted to scream, to shout, to hold him, to care for him all at once.

"I wish I was a better man for you," he said. Then he left.

CHAPTER 34

Saturday, December 12, 1987

M abel had told the boys that Bill was off to a trade show. She didn't have the courage to tell them their dad was trying to get sober again and wouldn't be back for a long time. While she had cried herself to sleep the last few nights and had canceled her diner shifts too, wishing she could stay home for weeks on end, her dinner with Dan and his mom was tonight and Mabel didn't have the heart to cancel that too. Her friend Consuela had picked the boys up earlier to watch them for the night, so Mabel started getting ready.

After several attempts to hide her tired eyes and blotchy cheeks, she put down her makeup brush and hoped they wouldn't notice. She got her hair right, with plenty of teasing and hairspray. But when she put on a dress, it reminded her of her last date with Bill a few weeks back, and she needed a tissue to dab her eyes so her mascara wouldn't run.

Dan's mother, Claudia, lived in a modest home that looked more worn since her husband had passed. It was a short drive away and Mabel parked on the road. With a bottle of Blue Nun white wine cradled in one arm, she knocked on the door.

Claudia's voice screeched from inside. "Dan! Get the door!"

Mabel exhaled slowly, expecting a long night. In preparation, she had asked Dan if his mom had many friends, and Dan replied sarcastically: "Who would want to?" And though Claudia was pleasant enough to meet on the street, she would always gossip about other women, which Mabel found exhausting.

Dan opened the door and Mabel forced a smile.

Dan tried to respond in kind, but his face was so tight that his smile failed miserably. She reached out to touch his arm, whispering, "It'll be fine."

Dan gave her a look like it would be a miracle.

Claudia screeched again. "Let her in! Know your manners boy!"

Mabel came in and took off her shoes.

Claudia was wearing an unflattering, shapeless multi-colored dress. Her hair was combed but not styled. "Mabel! So good to see you!" Claudia took her arm. "I'm glad you came. My Dannie says such nice things about you. But it's a shame he doesn't bring a nice girl home with him too. He's such a slow boy, and I think I'll be waiting forever for grandkids."

Dan turned a mottled red, so Mabel gave him a private, supportive look, as Claudia led them both into the kitchen.

Dan walked past them to the fridge. "I need a beer."

Claudia hit him hard. "You make sure your guests are settled first! Don't you go drinking first when Mabel doesn't have a drink yet." She turned to Mabel and smiled sweetly. "What would you like?"

"She brought wine, Mom."

"Oh, that's lovely." Claudia took the bottle from Mabel. "Oh, Blue Nun's Zin-fonion." Claudia mispronounced the name, but Mabel wasn't going to correct her. "How fancy. Look at this Dan, isn't that fancy?"

Dan nodded absently as he used the counter edge to snap off the beer cap.

"Don't be rude, boy! Pour her a glass!"

Dan's head bobbed up and down, and he did as asked. As he handed the wine to Mabel, she whispered, "It's going to be okay."

Claudia pulled out a chair. "Mabel, why don't you sit here and we can get started. I like to have dinner as soon as my guests arrive. My men like to eat first and socialize afterwards. Well, I guess it's just Dan now."

Mabel had never really had a chance to express her condolences to Claudia before, though it had been years. "I'm so sorry for your loss," she said, as Dan started to serve his own plate at the table.

"I miss him, everyday. It's strange being a widow. I'm not used to being on my own. But a widow is much better than being a divorcée or a single mom. Oh," she touched her mouth and looked at Mabel. "I'm sorry. I know you and Bill are … well, I'm sure you're used to people saying it."

"That's okay," Mabel said, biting back her real response. Women in this community feared being single or divorced, and Mabel learned to take these comments with a grain of salt.

Dan cleared his throat and asked, "Anyone want potatoes?"

"Of course, she wants potatoes," Claudia said, rolling her eyes at Mabel like her son was an idiot.

"Yes, please," Mabel said, not reacting to Claudia. "This looks wonderful," she added as the serving plates passed between them.

Claudia started the conversation off by gossiping about her neighbor, Beatrice, who was caught shoplifting at the Village Grocer.

Dan cut in, "You know we can't be discussing police business."

Claudia laughed, waving him off. "My Dannie tells me everything. And if you knew what some of the so-called respectable ladies are up to. Oh boy, makes you think they ain't so respectable behind closed doors if you know what I mean." She winked and laughed.

"Nobody is perfect," Mabel said, not wanting to judge anyone.

Claudia's smile fell slightly, and she replied, "Oh. Of course, you being a single mom and all, you know that. That must be so hard. I could never have raised a child on my own, let alone two. How are old are your boys now?"

"Twelve and nine."

Claudia tsked. "Young boys are meant to have a father. That's the Christian way."

Mabel tensed, struggling not to react. "Oh, they're doing fine," she said, scooping up some of her dinner.

"Your eldest isn't still getting into trouble with those Hudgens boys again, is he?"

Mabel's fork paused near her lips and she glanced at Dan, who looked away, embarrassed. Apparently, Dan shared gossip about her too. "No. They don't see Frank's kids no more."

Claudia laughed. "Now. Those two are a handful. The things I hear, oh Lord. Right Dannie? Why don't you tell us the latest goings on in town."

Dan wiped his mouth with a long pause like this would be it. He glanced at Mabel, who nodded at him encouragingly.

Claudia frowned, seeing the unspoken communication between them. "Well, spit it out," she said to Dan.

His cheeks flamed beet red. He roughly cleared his throat and then coughed, so he grabbed his beer and downed it. After setting it down, he burped quietly and turned awkwardly to face his mom.

Mabel watched, proud of him, but Claudia's face turned redder than Dan's.

"Well—" Dan started, then cleared his throat again.

"Go on! We ain't got all day."

Dan exhaled loudly and then said, just as quickly, "Kennie." But his nerves likely got the best of him as he just leaned over his plate, clenched his fists with arms resting on the table, and kept his head down.

"Kennie, what?" Claudia asked, angry now. "Why are you bringing *him* up?"

"Kennie and I are..." Dan glanced at Mabel, and she encouraged him with a nod.

Claudia's nostrils flared. "Are what! What's this?" She asked Mabel.

Then Dan spit it out in a rush. "Kennie and I are seeing each other."

Claudia's head cocked back like she was hit and her eyes widened and she leaned back in her chair till it tipped backwards.

Dan glanced at his mother quickly, then flinched and looked down, defeated.

Mabel jumped in. "Kennie's a good man Claudia and—"

Claudia held up her palm to Mabel. "Shut it!" Then she growled at Dan. "Don't do this, boy. Don't you do this! This isn't God's plan. This isn't you. You know what I think about that. How dare you tell me that, with company to boot! How dare you shame me like this!"

"Claudia, your son—"

"Don't you dare speak up! You think this is normal? Being a goddammed gay f—?" Her curse slashed them both. "I am a Christian mother. I run a Christian household. How dare you come into my home and encourage this … this … filth!"

Dan shrank deeper into his chair as Claudia got up and pointed her finger at him. "Don't you dare shame me! I am a good mother. You are a wicked, wicked son. Terrible! God will punish you for your sins, so help me—"

"Claudia!" Mabel shouted. "Your son is a good man. A hero. He saved me, this town, and—"

"How dare you talk to me! You did this! You! No wonder the town hates you! You and all your ungodly ways. Living alone in sin without a husband! Raising two feral boys! I should've known you would stoop to this. Get out! Out!"

Mabel flushed, furious with Claudia, but she turned to Dan, wanting to support him.

But then Claudia turned her wrath back on him. She hit him on the head, screaming, "Get her out of here!"

As Mabel got up to intervene, Dan got up too. Claudia kept slapping his back and shoulders, and Dan's face said it all. He wouldn't look at Mabel, but he led her out as Claudia kept screaming from the kitchen.

Dan ushered her to the door and when she stepped outside, she turned to Dan and whispered "I'm so sorry, Dan. That's so horrible. Whatever you need. I am here for you. I will stay if you need me."

"It's over, Mabel."

"But you and Kennie are good together. Don't listen to her!"

"It's over. We shouldn't be talking about this no more."

"But Dan!"

He shook his head and without looking back, he shut the door.

Claudia's screaming came through the solid wood and Mabel wanted to storm back in there to protect him, but she knew it would only make it worse. Never could she have imagined a mother treating her son so badly simply because he loved another man. It was terrible. Wrong. And Dan and Kennie were so good for each other and happy together. How could a mother wish otherwise?

She heard through the door Claudia's scream, "You're a disgrace!" Dan said something back that Mabel couldn't hear, and Claudia replied, "You better believe it!"

Then Mabel heard nothing more.

Overcome with sympathy for Dan, anger at Claudia, frustration at Bill, and everything in between, she squeezed her fists tight and cried, "Fuck!"

Then she bowed her head. "Oh Lord, please forgive me for my words, and..."

Ugh, she sighed.

"Fuck."

CHAPTER 35

Monday, December 14, 1987

It was 7 PM and the sparse diner crowd had mostly left. Mabel missed the over-the-top pace of last year when her place was packed with construction crews from the mine. She missed the energy, banter, and the lack of time to do anything but host and serve. Now, she had way too much time to think of what a mess her life was becoming. It had been almost a week since Bill had left and she had finally explained his unexpected departure to her disappointed sons. Hector turned angry, Fred went quiet and both reactions worried her. And then there was Dan. He hadn't returned any of her phone calls yesterday and she was worried sick about him. She hoped he wouldn't do anything rash like breaking up with Kennie.

The phone rang, and Mabel walked around the counter to pick it up, hoping it was either Bill or Dan. "Mabel speaking."

"I'm glad I caught you."

She covered her disappointment by forcing a cheery tone. "Lavi! How are you doing."

"How's our case going?"

With everything going on in her life, his expectation put her off until she reminded herself that he wouldn't know what she's dealing with. "Not much," she finally replied.

"You saw the mother, right?"

Mabel sighed and rubbed her neck. "Yes, and I got banned from the retirement home."

"What?" He chuckled. "That's a first. What's next?"

"What's next is that I have two boys to look after."

"Get Bill to look after them. We've got the trial coming up."

"He's not here, Lavi," she replied in a tone that said it all.

"Oh."

She waited for any sort of sympathetic comment, but when none came, she asked, frustrated, "That's it? Just, 'oh?'"

"Look, I'm sorry about Bill, but this is important. We need plausible evidence that someone else could have done it."

"I'm not an investigator, no matter what you tell me. I talked to Angelica and then my suspect. It's a dead end. I don't know what else to do."

"You talked to Mr. Ketch?"

"Briefly, but that didn't go well either."

"What did John Ford say then?"

Mabel covered her eyes, wanting to quit, but her promise to Patty and Kelly forced her hand. "Fine. I'll talk to him again." She sighed. "I'm also thinking of looking into Samuel's father that passed. Maybe there was something more behind it, I don't know. Kerry gave me that lead. Maybe that will generate something new."

"O-kay," Lavi said, sounding unconvinced. "But I think there's more you can do here and—"

"I got to go. Customers," she cut him off and hung up.

Mabel leaned against the counter, feeling bad for lying, but everything was just so depressing, she didn't have the energy to argue. With the boys sleeping over at a friend's house, she'd have even more time to stew over her problems, and she'd done enough of that already.

She looked around the diner, newly decorated by Sally and Molly for the upcoming Christmas holidays, but it didn't cheer her mood as it usually did. Only two people were left, one rooting for his wallet, the other sitting in the farthest booth. He must have arrived while she was on the phone, and with his head down, wearing a baseball cap, probably a tired trucker coming off a long route. She'd already sent Kevin home, figuring dinner was done, and had planned to pack up early so she could drown her sorrows in a few glasses of wine. But that would have to wait. She attempted to fix a friendly smile, but when that failed miserably, she gave that up and hoped she didn't look too miserable walking over.

As she approached, the man lifted his cap slightly and she caught a glimpse of a mustache and a glint in his dark eyes.

The hairs on her neck rose, but she did not know why.

When she reached the table to hand him a menu, she gasped—

The menu slipped through her fingers, landing on the table.

"Hello, Mabel," Samuel Ketch said with a smile.

A terrified Mabel quickly glanced over her shoulder to see if she was alone. The last customer was dropping money on the table for the bill.

"I told you I'd come."

Mabel's throat constricted as she gasped, "W-what are you doing here?"

"You talked to my mother. I didn't like that."

The other customer was walking to the door. With her heart racing, she demanded, "What do you want?"

"You wanted to talk to me. So, talk."

The door chimed twice.

Alone now. With him.

She quelled the urge to flee because this was her diner. And no one, not Larson, not Samuel, could keep her from being in control here.

He gestured for her to sit.

She sat down, suppressing a chilling shudder.

He took his time to glance around before he said, "This place hasn't changed."

She pushed back regardless of her fear. "I know you used to visit here with your mother."

He smiled. "Is that all you remember?"

She hesitated, confused, and then explained, "It was Kyle who first told me about you."

He frowned. "Who's Kyle?"

"A Larson man."

"Ahh," he nodded like he understood now. "He worked for Karl Larson then. Of course." He smiled. "How is our friend Karl doing?"

"He's no friend of mine. But he's in prison, where I put him," she said with a bravado she did not feel.

Samuel examined her for a breathless minute. "I wondered," he said, at last. "I read the papers. And they hinted about some private investigator and a lawyer … Arron or Abraham or something." Mabel didn't correct him. "Then of course, the *Seattle Times* article about Paul Hammetts told me more about you. But I don't remember who this Kyle is."

"He said you started that horrid place. The coop, they call it."

He nodded slowly as he turned a knife around on his napkin so the blade pointed at her, steel glinting. "You know, Karl didn't have his heart in it. He only played at the game."

"You don't deny it then?"

He smiled to himself. "That was a long time ago. More has happened since."

"Is this a confession?"

He scoffed. "I haven't been to church for years, not since my mother forced me to go every Sunday. A horrid woman."

"But you take care of her."

He nodded. "You might be surprised to hear this, but I like you. You are not like the police. They talked to me, you know. Said they were following up on a lead and I think that lead came from you. Am I right?" Mabel didn't say anything, but he read her and nodded. Then smiled again. "You came to see my mother and opened a door into my life again whether you wanted to or not. You know who she is and what I had to endure." A brief flash of rage showed in his eyes before he mastered it again. "But that won't last long."

"Why?" Mabel asked, breathless.

"I know you're alone tonight."

"W-what do you want with me?"

He stood up and she did too, ready to run.

His gaze held hers with such intensity that she stepped backwards, so terrified she couldn't breathe.

Then, after savoring her discomfort, he walked out without another word.

CHAPTER 36

Thursday, December 17, 1987

Kevin had walked the still-shaken Mabel home the last few nights since Samuel had visited the diner. With the boys over at a friend's birthday sleepover, only the red emergency lights were on in the parking lot and those did little but cast deep shadows. The enveloping forest was pitch-black as always and offered no comfort. She thanked Kevin and then waited on the porch as he drove off, her anxiety increasing as his car's taillights bled away and the last of its engine noises faded into eerie silence.

Alone.

As she turned to go in, a distant wolf howled, and she panicked and rushed inside.

The snap of the deadbolt calmed her somewhat, but the house was as dark as the forest. Colder than usual, too. She shivered and rubbed her arms. Suspecting her boys had left a window open, she headed upstairs without taking off her jacket, turning on every light to find it. As she got closer to the office, it grew colder still.

That's strange, she thought.

She turned on the desk lamp.

The office window latch had broken the day before and she had tied it down with twine, but the twine was cut and the window wide open. She wound the latch closed and then searched her desk for more string to tie it back down.

Turning to face the cabinet, she caught sight of the wallboard and screamed.

Twelve of the remaining missing girls' images had red and white makeup grotesquely smeared on them. Someone had been here. Someone was inside her home.

Mabel pressed her back against the wall, expecting an intruder to rush in at any moment. Seeing the phone, she grabbed it and dialed frantically, each ring seemingly taking forever.

"Hiya, this is Sheriff Dan—"

"Dan!"

"—Gibson. If this is police business, leave a message."

Mabel swore.

The machine beeped to leave a message. "Dan!" she cried frantically. "Someone was here. I think he's been in my home! Hurry. Come quick, please. I'm all alone."

Outside, her compound was dark except for the lone emergency lights shining like red eyes.

No one else was around for miles.

She slapped the light off in her office and the one in the hall to put her second floor into darkness.

A strange noise sounded downstairs, creeping her out.

"Don't worry," she whispered aloud to herself, breathless. "No one's here. Dan's coming and—"

Thump.

Her heart nearly burst out of her chest.

She ran to her bedroom, covering her mouth to stop from screaming, and then closed the door but for a gap to listen.

A bottom stair creaked.

She shut the door and locked it. But the lock was one even her kids could pick with a pen. She backed up, looking for any weapon. Bill's side of the bed was empty and cold, the rifle underneath that he kept for bear protection was gone with him.

She was defenseless.

"Damn it, Bill," she whispered to herself. "I need you."

He was so good at protecting her, so conscious of safety protocols drilled into him from work that he—

The ladders, she remembered. He kept a rope ladder in each of the upstairs closets in case of fire. She opened her closet, pushed off a stack of clothes from the unused ladder box, and pulled the coil out. Then rushed to her window.

A creaking step in her hallway.

She whimpered with fear, then cranked the window open, shakily attaching the ladder hooks to the windowsill. Then tossed the rungs out like Bill had taught her, and the ladder uncoiled with a snap, and then banged loudly against the house.

Pounding steps rushed toward her door.

Her scream burst through her hands.

The door shook, the knob rattled.

Mabel put her leg out the window but froze as the ground rushed up dizzyingly. Terrified of heights, she backed away.

Loud bangs against her door forced her out.

The flimsy, swaying ladder was hard to hold, and she nearly slipped and fell. She grasped and clutched the rungs in terror, but near bottom, her foot slipped, and she fell, screaming, landing hard. Pain shot up her leg and she collapsed.

Looking up past the flapping curtains of her bedroom, she saw the dark outline of a man.

Mabel whimpered, crawling backward. Then she staggered up. Her ankle hurt terribly, but she hobbled on, glancing back in terror, imagining a man running through her house to get outside.

She stumbled on as fast as she could to her car. Then she padded her jacket pockets for her keys; but they were the motel keys, not for the car. She cursed and pushed off its hood, hobbling into the open hallway between the diner and the motel. Clutching the railing, she clawed up the stairs to the second floor, weeping in pain.

Her ankle kept giving way, and she gritted her teeth to pull herself along the wall to the third room down. The open hallway exposed her to the gravel lot, the diner, her house behind.

Heavy footfalls in the gravel meant he was getting closer. Her shaking hands dropped the motel keys. She scooped them up and then shoved the right key in, opened the door and collapsed inwards, locking it behind her.

She pressed her back to the door, gulping in deep breaths.

The darkness inside exposed the trap she put herself in. There was no way out.

She pushed off the door to land on the dresser and then dragged it back to block the door. The phone fell off with a loud clang, and she cursed it.

She grabbed the phone by its cord and dragged it towards her. The dial tone sounded, and she dialed Dan's number again. Tears flooded her eyes as she willed him to answer. His voice machine came on, and she whimpered.

The beep sounded.

Mabel whispered as loud as she dared, "Dan! Please! Help me. Someone's here. I am in room 208 in the motel. Please! Come quick!"

The hall light winked out, and she covered her mouth to stop a scream.

A shadow darted past the curtains.

Then her doorknob started to turn slowly.
Then rattle violently.
Thump!
Her door shook.
Thump! Thump!
Her scream escaped her hands.

CHAPTER 37

A distant whoop, whoop of a police cruiser siren grew louder and soon the glow of red and blue lights flashed across her curtains.

Mabel, with her back pressed to the clothes dresser used to blockade the motel door, screamed, "Dan!" Then she edged the dresser out of the way, unlocked the door, and squeezed herself through, screaming his name over and over until he responded.

"Oh my God, what happened!" Dan shouted as he got out of his cruiser in the motel parking lot.

"He was here! He was here!"

"Who?"

"Someone was in my home! I think it was Samuel!"

"Jesus," he said, pulling out his gun. He came huffing up the stairs and then peeked into the motel room and quickly scanned the out of place dresser and the phone on the floor.

Mabel hurriedly told him what had happened.

A stunned Dan shook his head. "Come on then," he said, grimly. "Let's check it out."

Her leg hurt terribly so Dan holstered his gun and guided her down the stairs. His cruiser lights illuminated the motel and diner in flashing colors.

Mabel paused at the electrical junction, opened it with her motel keychain and then Dan flipped all the breakers. As the entire parking lot flooded in light, the neon motel and diner sign flickered before it shone bright red, buzzing in the night.

Rounding the corner to her home, she could see right away that the rope ladder out of her bedroom was in a heap on the ground. "He must have pushed it out," she said, but Dan was silent.

When they made it to her front porch, he peeked into her den window before they entered and turned on every light again as they went. He called out a warning at each turn and checked each room. But there were no signs of disturbance until she led him into the office.

She gasped. "They were here! I promise you!"

The defaced photos of the girls were gone. "I saw it, Dan! They were here and now they're gone!" Then she showed him her bedroom door, but there was no damage, and after he bent down to double check the lock, he stood up, doubtful. She could see he didn't believe her and so she pleaded, "Someone was here! They were banging against this door! I mean it!"

The doubt and anger in his eyes hurt terribly.

She did her best to stem the tears before she hobbled over to her bed and then collapsed down, rubbing her ankle from the pain.

Dan crossed his arms, and the long silence between them made it worse. She didn't look up, feeling ill from the fading terror and the guilt for hurting their friendship that night with Dan's mom.

Finally, he asked, angry and tense like she was wasting his time, "Where are the boys?"

"At a friend's house."

"And Bill?"

Her tone said it all, "He's gone."

Dan's face softened and then he uncrossed his arms as if he didn't know where to put them. He said, finally, "I'm sorry ... I truly am." He lumbered over and sat down, crushing the bed beside her.

She glanced over, and then nodded, depressed. "I'm sorry too. That dinner, it…" But she left it hanging, not knowing where to start.

"That dinner…" Dan echoed. "Didn't do any good."

"How did Kennie take it?"

Dan took off his hat and used his fist to push out an indent. "We're done."

"Oh, Dan, no! I'm so sorry. What happened?"

Dan struggled to talk for a moment. Then his voice broke as he said, "I ended it."

"Why?"

He paused for a long moment before wiping his welling eyes and then grumbled, "Ugh, you leaving the window open makes my eyes water from the cold." He hmphed and half-smiled to make it clear he knew he wasn't convincing anyone. He cleared his throat roughly before he added, serious again, "I promised ma."

"Dan! You deserve to be happy! He makes you happy and—"

He put his palm up to stop her and said, "Mabel! You see what it's like for people like us. What even my ma thinks of me. It's best it's over. For him. For us."

"But he makes you happy."

Dan's face twisted in pain, and so Mabel touched his arm. When he didn't stiffen, she gave him a hug. After a time, he leaned into her before he broke down completely and cried.

"Your mom is wrong, you know," she said softly, rubbing his back.

Dan wiped his eyes, his voice breaking. "She's no different than anyone else in this town. If they knew about us, well, I wouldn't be the sheriff no more and Kennie'd lose his job."

"But you'd be together."

Dan dropped his head, nodding, and whispered, "There'd be that."

She examined him. "We are a pair, aren't we?"

He nodded, and since both were too depressed to laugh, they only smiled wanly at each other.

"So, uh, Bill he…" Dan asked.

She rubbed her hurt ankle again to give herself time to frame her answer. Then nodded. "Drinking again."

"Hmph."

"Yeah. But he came clean about it, though."

Dan brightened. "That's something."

"That's something," she echoed.

They both went silent, brooding together.

Then Dan exhaled loudly, and added, looking around, "I think we can get some Staties in. Maybe some detectives too to check for fingerprints and such."

'Thanks Dan," she said with emotion.

He nodded shyly and then looked away.

"You didn't answer any of my calls all this week," she said, her voice breaking from hurt. "But I guess you just answer the most important ones. Thank you, Dan. You are my hero."

He reddened, embarrassed.

Then he gave her a look. "I'd tell you to stop investigating, but you don't seem to listen. So, how about this? Let's just not have any more dinners with my ma, okay?"

CHAPTER 38

Friday, December 18, 1987

The state police officer who'd come by near midnight had called for some detectives to stop by in the morning. Dan rested on the couch in the den to keep Mabel safe, but neither slept that night.

By 6 AM she crawled out of bed and made Dan coffee and breakfast.

Two hours later, they were still in the kitchen, nursing a third cup of coffee each and saying little, when Detectives Sue Tomlinson and Todd Smith arrived — the same investigators who had interviewed Mabel about Paul Hammetts. Mabel walked them through what happened last night, and then took them upstairs to show them the evidence. When she pointed out potential places to take fingerprints, they just thanked her and moved past. That irked Mabel, but she kept on, hoping their skeptical attitudes would change.

Detective Smith checked her bedroom lock and Mabel thought she could see scratch marks on the knob, but he couldn't. She showed him the office next. Then she told them about the twelve makeup-smeared photos, now gone, and named which had been defaced, noting that could be a clue they were victims of the Dollhouse Killer.

Detective Sue Tomlinson sounded bored. "We have a suspect in custody, ma'am. Trust me, he's going to be in prison a very long time."

"But he's the wrong man! Paul's in jail and couldn't have done this," Mabel said, her frustrations getting the best of her. "It's Samuel Ketch, I told you. He was here."

"You're working for Mr. Arronson, right? The public defender for Paul Hammetts, our suspect?"

"Well. Yes."

Detective Tomlinson raised her eyebrows to her partner and said to Mabel, "You don't think it's a coincidence that a PI working for the public defender gets targeted. Isn't that a little too far-fetched?"

"It's true!"

"Uh-huh," the detective said, unimpressed. "You said the perp chased you to the motel?" Mabel nodded. "Did you see what he looked like?"

"No. I didn't see him. But Samuel Ketch was in my diner four days ago!"

"Four days." She glanced at her partner. "Anything missing, ma'am?"

"Makeup," Mabel said. "I'm missing some makeup. I think he used it on those pictures."

"You got robbed of makeup? No money, jewelry, TV? Nothing of value stolen?" Mabel was forced to shake her head. "Okay." The detective flipped her notebook closed.

"Don't you want to see the motel?"

"Sure," the detective drawled, unimpressed. "Why not?"

Feeling very unappreciated and with her leg still hurting, she marched them across the lot to show them the motel. Detective Tomlinson glanced inside and only raised her eyebrows upon seeing the moved dresser and phone of the floor, but she had no questions. Her partner bent down and examined the door lock. "Ain't broke," he said.

"I didn't say it was," Mabel protested.

Detective Tomlinson sighed. "Ma'am. I going to talk to the sheriff outside here a second. You wait here with Detective Smith." Then the detective went downstairs to talk with Dan, who was leaning against his cruiser, picking his teeth.

As Detective Smith casually went through the motions of looking throughout the room, Mabel crossed her arms and stood outside in the second-floor breezeway to listen to Detective Tomlinson talk to Dan below.

"You came by when?" Detective Tomlinson asked Dan, but Dan's voice was too low to hear. "You see the perp?" Dan shook his head. "Okay. No cars in the lot? He couldn't just run right? Is anything close?" Dan shook his head again. "Has she been known to call in any false alarms?"

Mabel shouted down. "I ain't making this up!"

Detective Tomlinson ignored Mabel before listening to Dan's spirited response while Mabel hobbled downstairs to the cruiser, furious they didn't believe her.

"It did happen!" Mabel said.

Detective Tomlinson put her palm up. "Ma'am. I'm doing an investigation here."

Detective Smith came down too so Detective Tomlinson asked him, "Find anything?" He shook his head and Mabel huffed.

"Okay, ma'am. Here's the thing. You're working for the public defender on the Hammetts case. You're also calling in another potential perp who you *say* stole makeup from your home and is actually the real killer."

Mabel crossed her arms angrily and then nodded.

Detective Tomlinson turned to her partner. "Go around and get the car." Then she said to Mabel, "I have to do the paperwork on this because that's our policy. But please don't waste my time."

"You mean if he breaks into my home again and tries to kill me? I can call you and if I'm still alive, you'll show up the next day?"

"Seems you got the sheriff here on your side. But you also got some local hooligans leaving dolls and such. They're probably just trying to scare you again."

Mabel was about to protest when Dan motioned Mabel to back off and she bit back her response.

Detective Tomlinson said to Dan, "I'll write this up quick and give you a copy." Then she looked at Mabel. "Two hours out of our day impacts more serious investigations. I hope you'll think about that next time."

Dan immediately stepped in front of Mabel before she could respond. He whispered, "I got it."

Mabel fumed but did as she was told.

Detective Tomlinson got into the driver's seat and used the steering wheel as a writing board as Mabel unleashed her anger with Dan, "Can you believe this?"

Dan guided her away and said gruffly, "I'm sorry. But you being an investigator on the Hammetts thing doesn't help. There's no evidence of a break-in apparent here."

"Someone was in my home!"

"I believe you. I do. But look at it from their perspective." She was about to cut in, but he added, quickly, "I'm not saying she's right, I'm not. I'll be around and make sure I stop by as much as I can, okay?" Then he paused and asked, "Any chance you can get word to Bill? Having a man around for protection would be a big help."

Mabel shook her head, thinking Bill was no use to her or the kids if he was sobering up.

"Kerry is coming home for Christmas," she said instead.

"Better to have a man around, but at least you won't be alone with the boys. Like I said, I'll stop by and park here as much as I can."

She was still angry, but it wasn't Dan's fault so she put her hand on his shoulder and said, "Thanks."

"I'm here for you, Mabel. I promise ya."

She nodded and then scanned the tall cliffs and dark forest around her, knowing Dan couldn't be here all the time. She whispered under her breath, "I'll just have to protect myself."

CHAPTER 39

Mabel was behind her diner counter, one hand on her hip, the other holding the phone, while she surveyed her customers. "I got some news for you," she said into the receiver.

"Shoot," replied John Ford.

"Someone invaded my home last night."

"Oh, Jesus!"

"State detectives showed up but didn't believe me."

"Why?"

"I'm doing investigative work for the public defender, Lavi Arronson. He's representing Paul Hammetts."

"The Dollhouse Killer?"

"That's what he's charged with. But he doesn't fit the profile. He's not white and preys on much younger girls."

"But if he's in jail, how does this break-in relate to your case?"

Mabel faced away from her customers and lowered her voice. "Because Paul Hammetts couldn't have been here. But get this, Samuel Ketch came to visit me four days back. Came right here to my diner. And then, all of a sudden, a few days later someone breaks into my home. Chases me to my motel. Takes things. It's scary."

John was silent for a moment and then said, "Listen to me. This is serious. Be careful what you do. Are you sure the detectives didn't believe you?"

"They didn't even take fingerprints."

"Well, that's understandable. But if I was them, I would interview Samuel Ketch. Do you think they will?"

"I don't know. As far as I know, they're not planning to."

"You need to get off that Paul Hammetts case then. If there's no conflict of interest, those detectives might take you more seriously," Ford said. "They should also talk to Samuel. At the very least, it might make him back off knowing he's being watched. Who are the detectives?" Mabel told him. "Okay, I'll give the lead a call."

"They're also investigating the case against Paul Hammetts."

John tsked. "They may not be open to a new suspect then. Do you feel safe out there? What did he do? What did he take exactly?"

Mabel told him.

"He took your makeup, you sure?" Mabel said yes and then John sounded more serious. "I'll be honest. That's not a good sign. They take trophies of their victims, but it is usually after the fact." She heard him click a pen repeatedly. "Hmmm, his first attempt at you was unsuccessful, but he may try again. Normally, once they get scared off, they hunt someone else. While Samuel is behaving to type, we have to be cautious. A profile is a model, and models are never perfect. He will have deviations. Is there someone who can watch over your home?"

"The local sheriff is going to try to drive by more."

"Ask him to come at night — these killers have preferred times. Samuel's, it seems, is at night. You have two boys, right?"

"Twelve and nine." Her voice cracked. "Do you think he'll go after them?"

After a longer pause that terrified Mabel, John's words came as a relief, "No. That's not his preferred gender or age. But I would still see if your boys could stay at a friend's house for a few days, at least. Your suspect, if the detectives don't question him, may think he is in the clear and he could try again. These men are very meticulous and detail oriented. You said he confronted you inside the diner. What did he say?"

"He said he knew I was alone. My husband left recently, and I don't know how he knows this."

John exhaled. "That's not good either. Those pictures and your makeup he took tell me he's marked you. I'm not trying to say this to scare you but is there any way you can take a few days off. Stay with relatives out of town?"

"I have a business. Christmas is coming and it's one of our busiest times. I can't leave."

"Of course, okay. I'll call the detectives and tell them that you're off the Hammetts case. It might help soften them to the fact you're being targeted by this man," he said. "Keep your chin up. And get some protection."

She agreed and they hung up.

Mabel pressed her palm to her chest to calm herself before dialing Lavi.

"Arronson," Lavi said after the fourth ring.

Mabel dived in to tell him the same updates she had told John. When she told Lavi she needed to leave the Hammetts case, she expected a protest, but he surprised her.

"I agree. You're off this case," Lavi said. "If those detectives think you're making false statements for my client's benefit, they certainly don't know you. I'm going to call them. I don't care what assumptions they have, they need to protect you." His fierceness heartened her more. "I'm also going to organize security for you in Blue River." He paused, sounding like he was flipping a calendar. "Okay, it's Friday now.

I'll have a security man out first thing Monday morning. Can you make sure you're either not at home or have a friend stay with you until then?"

"My niece Kerry is coming home from college tonight. She'll be here over Christmas holidays. My boys will stay at a friend's place. They'll be fine. Oh, and the sheriff. He'll try to hang out in the parking lot at night."

"That should be enough for now. No one comes after my investigators. I mean that."

"Thanks," Mabel said, her relief coming in a wave.

"No problem. I'm on it. Monday morning, you'll get a full-time security detail until we nab this killer. You'll be protected, and I'll get another investigator on Ketch. Talk soon, I've got calls to make." Then he hung up.

Mabel closed her eyes, feeling better already. She grabbed a pot of coffee and strode around serving customers like a weight had been lifted from her shoulders. With the police presence and Lavi's security men, she'd be safe. If Samuel Ketch thought he could scare her, he had another thing coming.

CHAPTER 40

A untie!" Kerry cried out.

Mabel rushed down the porch to give Kerry a big hug. Then she took Kerry's backpack, which was surprisingly light, and guided her in from the cold.

Kerry paused, breathing in the smells of home, before Hector and Fred came barreling down the stairs, almost knocking her over with their hugs. Kerry laughed and ruffled Fred's hair; then she reached into her bag and sang, "I brought presents!"

Fred jumped up and down with glee. Kerry pulled out comic books for Fred and some dark sunglasses for Hector, who promptly tried them on. After admiring himself in the mirror, he struck a cool pose and then raised his eyebrows repeatedly above the rims. Mabel and Kerry laughed before complimenting him, and

Hector seemed to stand a little taller. "Don't worry," Kerry added. "I have your real gifts still in the car."

Mabel gave Kerry another big hug. "Ohhh, it's so good to see you! I have your room all set up, of course. New sheets and everything. It's so good to have you home."

Kerry laughed and then asked the boys to take her to her room. The three headed upstairs, Kerry taking each of their questions in stride and trying to answer them all.

Mabel sighed happily and went back to the kitchen to finish cooking, then called them to the table. "Boys! Kerry! Dinner!"

They raced downstairs and jumped into their usual seats.

During the meal, Kerry regaled them with tales of college life, and Mabel couldn't help but think what a grown woman she was. Her hair was done up, and she was wearing the latest blouse and baggy trouser fashion you might see on MTV. She was even wearing blush and eyeliner, and she looked beautiful.

After dessert, Mabel took command. "Okay, boys. Do you have your bags packed for the weekend?" They nodded. "Fred, do you have your pajamas?" He nodded. "Hector, do you have an extra set of pants?" He nodded as well. "Okay then, go get your stuff, and let's go." Both boys raced off but collided on the stairs and started fighting the rest of the way.

Mabel rolled her eyes at the constant battles and turned to see Kerry smile. "You sure you don't mind driving them over to Michelle's?" Mabel asked. "You spent the last hour-and-a-half on the road to get here, and I don't mind taking them over if you want a rest."

Kerry gave her a sly look. "Well, Lisa's in town. So … if you don't mind, I'd like to visit her too after dropping off the boys. We have lots to catch up on and I want to see her engagement ring."

Mabel groaned inwardly, as she had planned a quiet evening of girl talk, but she covered her disappointment well. "I know! She's marrying my cook, Kevin. That rascal! How dare they!" Mabel laughed to show no ill will. "Kevin's over the moon with Lisa, and they seem such a good couple."

"I've only talked to her a few times on the phone, but she sounds happy. I like boys too, but I'd say that's really fast."

Mabel paused after catching an underlying meaning. "Are you dating now too?"

Kerry blushed, tight-lipped for only the briefest moment before it rushed out. "He's a sophomore taking pre-med. Straight A's. Athletic. Oh, so-o-o delicious!"

Mabel's voice took on a higher pitch. "When did you start dating?"

"After I dumped Davis."

"Who's Davis!?"

"Oh, my previous boyfriend. But he was too into himself. Star football quarterback and all that. I dumped him."

"Star quarterback, two boyfriends, dear ... Why didn't you tell me? We talk every week."

"Oh, no big deal."

"No! It is a very big deal! You're such a grown woman now. We're going to have so much to catch up on!"

Kerry gave a little pose, blushing, and then broke out laughing. Then she grabbed Mabel's arms and shook her. "I just love, love, love college, Auntie! I can't tell you how much fun it is!"

"Well, tell me something about it as the boys are getting ready."

Kerry pulled Mabel into the den, and they flopped down on the couch next to the Christmas tree. Kerry curled up with her legs underneath, and Mabel sat beside her. She poured a glass of red wine and offered Kerry a small glass to see how she would react, hoping she wouldn't be interested, but Kerry accepted with only a slight blush and sipped like she was comfortable with it. This girl was growing up too quickly!

After they talked some more about her latest boyfriend, they turned serious, discussing Bill's alcoholic relapse and what happened with Samuel Ketch. Kerry shivered, crossing her arms. "I'm so glad Dan's parked out by the diner. I can't believe you had some creep in here. Do the boys know?"

"Not yet. Only you."

Kerry looked around the place. "It's so weird he took your makeup and walked around in here. That's scary!"

Mabel nodded, swirling her wine around before taking a sip. "I'm getting security protection on Monday. And Dan said he'd be out front for as much as he could till then. Even John Ford's trying to get the state detectives to scare off Samuel Ketch, so I don't think he will try anything again."

Kerry shook her head, taking a sip. Then shifted her legs to the other side, and said, "It's so cool you're working with the FBI again. That's my ambition, you know."

"You still have that mentor of yours?"

"Yeah, Mr. Jacob's been good to me. He even recommended some courses I should take, and I did. I guess the feds have a big need for forensic accountants, and he says if I get good grades, I could probably get hired after graduation." She shrugged like it was no big deal. Then her cool broke down and she laughed.

"A career and everything," Mabel shook her head, amazed and proud. "Your parents would be so proud. Especially your dad."

Kerry's eyes welled up thinking about her parents' deaths just two years earlier, and Mabel's heart went out to her.

"I'm sorry," Mabel said.

Kerry waved her off to dab her eyes with a tissue.

"I wish I could make things right for you."

Kerry's voice broke at first but then grew stronger. "You are. And I know how hard I was on you when I first came." Mabel brushed that off, but Kerry kept on.

"And I want to thank you for everything you've done. I know my mom would be so happy you're here for me."

They reached out to hold hands, enjoying the moment, until the boys tore downstairs, still roughhousing. Mabel yelled, "No fighting!" and she and Kerry exchanged a rueful look. "You sure you can handle these two?"

Kerry chuckled, and then said loudly for the boys to hear, as she pantomimed karate moves, "I've got some secret FBI moves to whip them into shape."

The boys stopped cold.

"Cool!" Fred said.

"It's time!" Mabel said, looking at the clock. "Get your jackets on."

She gave a hug and kiss to both boys, with only Hector pretending like he didn't need it, and then hugged Kerry and added, "Can't wait for more talks this weekend!"

"Me too! Especially about the case." Kerry smiled. Then added slyly, glancing at the red wine in the den. "But I prefer white if you have it."

"Oh, you scoundrel!"

Kerry laughed as she left.

Mabel stood proudly at the door to watch the car back out and then stop by Dan's cruiser. Kerry then rolled down the window to talk briefly to Dan before she waved back to Mabel and peeled out of the lot.

Mabel grabbed a jacket and put on winter boots to walk to the cruiser. When Dan rolled down the window again, a blast of heat hit her, and she asked, "You sure you don't want to come in? I can feed you dinner."

Dan shook his head and pointed to the radio. "Kathy is on the switchboard tonight. I'm on call till 4 AM and I gotta stay close to this thing. Shouldn't be a problem, though. Not much goes on out here anymore."

"Well, that won't stop me from feeding you," she said. "I'll swing by with a lasagna and a few cookies later. Do you want coffee too?"

"Don't mind if I do," he said, smiling.

"I'll ask Molly to keep an eye out on ya as well and top you up regular before she leaves. How's that sound?"

"You sure know how to treat a man."

Mabel thought of Bill, and that pained her, so she said, "You make me feel safe, Dan. I appreciate you."

Dan blushed as he mumbled, "Don't mention it."

She left to go to the diner to talk to Molly and then loaded up a picnic basket with two servings of lasagna, salad, cookies, and a thermos of coffee and carted it back to the cruiser.

Dan leaned over to unlock the passenger side door and then did his best to pick up all the discarded food wrappers and toss them into the backseat. While she would have preferred a washed seat too, she let it be and got in.

The radio squawked, but it wasn't for Dan. The heat was blasting, and Mabel unzipped her coat, sweating.

"That smells good," Dan said, licking his lips, as she popped the lid off the containers and then handled him a salad and lasagna. "Hey! What's with all the greens? Takes up all the prime real estate on my plate."

"Oh, hush Dan. Eat your salad."

He chuckled before he picked up his cutlery to dig in.

Then she popped the question she'd been dying to ask. "You talked to Kennie, yet?"

Dan's face fell and his enthusiasm waned. He only toyed with his food now, and Mabel did the same, not sure if Dan wanted to talk or not, and regretted bringing it up.

His eyes started to well and he wiped them roughly. "God Mabel, you make everyone around ya so emotional. Crying all the time, caring about people, it's terrible!" Then he half-smiled to show her no harm.

He toyed with his food one last time before he finally put it down and turned serious again. "But here's what I've been thinking. Look at you. You rid this town of a great evil, and half the place is mad at you. But as many that are mad at you for that, double would hate me for just being me. Same with Kennie. They'd hate him too. I'm not ignorant. I'm not deaf to all the jokes about my weight behind my back and such. But I grew a thick skin from that. I can handle it. But Kennie, he, uh, he ain't like that. He's sensitive and kind and ain't like me. Now, I'd shoot the legs off someone who might treat him bad. I would have to shoot practically the entire town if we told people we were … you know. I'm not seeing Kennie because I don't ... you know, care for him, but—"

"You can say love."

"Ugh, would you just..." Dan paused and gave her a look to stop and she raised her palms up to show him she would. "I know what you're trying to do here, but Kennie and me are freaks—" Mabel started to protest, but he stopped her with a look. "We are. Look at my mom, my dad. I grew up hearing how much they hated the gays. And anytime I showed any interest in boys, they said it was a sin. They threw God in my face and told me that all gays go to hell." Dan shifted in his seat. "I think ... I think my mom always knew what I am. And it scared her. Hell, it scared me. I didn't want to be different. I tried not to. That's why I went into policing, thinking if I'd be a real man, and forget these things, she'd accept me. But—" his voice failed him, and he struggled to talk. "But when I, uh, met Kennie ... that all changed. And when he showed interest in me back, I ..." He stopped and smiled. But then his smile slowly fell, and his face contorted in pain. "But you don't go against your parent's wishes. You know that. That's the Blue River way. And I can't be what I am 'cause if I do, my mom will disown me. She raised me and I can't disrespect that.

"Screw that," Mabel said, not caring about swearing — she'd straighten it up with God later. "What she said to you was horrible. What no mom should say to a son."

"But she's my mom, and I need you to stop talking about Kennie and me. It's over. I'll just go back to being the sheriff and he'll be with the Staties and we'll leave it at that."

"What about your happiness?"

Dan sighed and looked out at the distant blue-gray mountain in the night, stars twinkling on high. "Over-rated," he said finally, offering the barest hint of a smile like it was a joke.

"You are worth it, Dan Gibson. You are!"

But Dan was done. He shut down by taking a bite of his lasagna and eased back in his seat, and while Mabel wanted to keep talking, now wasn't the right time. Instead, she huffed loudly to make sure he knew how unhappy she was with how this conversation ended and took a small bite herself.

"Tastes good, doesn't it?" Dan asked, his mouth full.

"Don't you sweet talk me!"

Dan started laughing until he choked, and she pounded his back until he finally cleared it with a sip of coffee. She said, "Oh Dan, what am I going to do with you?"

Dan eased into his seat further, and said, "You know something? This place is a paradise. It is. The mountains, the woods, the hunting, and the like. And you and me will never leave it. But right now, folks in this town hate people like me and Kennie, and like that Winston of yours. But maybe, someday, if opinion changes, if people change, then maybe people like

Winston can live here proper and Kennie and me can be together again."

"I pray for that. Every day."

Dan nodded. "With that, I agree wholeheartedly."

CHAPTER 41

Mabel's feet were up on her den's coffee table and she had a glass of red wine in hand, watching Dan Rather on CBS news. It was well past 10 PM when Kerry said she'd be coming home, and Mabel was staying up to make sure she got home safely.

A siren whooped and the cruiser's lights flashed in the dimly lit parking lot, startling her. She put her glass down hurriedly and ran to open the front door.

The chilled air made her grab her coat to wrap around her shoulders as Dan shouted, half-out of his cruiser, "Got an emergency! A fire out by the Cresdon farm!"

Mabel waved him on. "You go on! Kerry should be home soon."

"Lock that door! And make sure you call Kathy every half hour."

Dan got back in his cruiser and spun it off the gravel and onto the highway, illuminating the dark forest in flashes of red and blue before disappearing around the bend.

When all the commotion died down, the surrounding snow-covered woods seemed eerily still.

Mabel shivered and wrapped her coat tighter. A bank of clouds moved in front of the moon, intensifying the deep darkness around her.

Alone again.

Mabel turned to walk back up her porch steps, but a surge of fear rushed her up the last steps and she banged the door shut, exhaling only when the deadbolt clicked. The house was well lit, with the Christmas tree lights twinkling. But with no boys around, the home was as silent as the dark woods outside.

She returned to the den to wait for Kerry, but her wine bottle and glass were empty, and she needed a little more fortified courage. She dropped off the empty bottle in the kitchen and opened the basement door to get another. But when she flipped the light switch at the top of the stairs, the same surge of fear she had felt at her doorstep returned. The steps leading down were even more claustrophobic now, and the wood framed concrete walls were covered in dusty cobwebs she hadn't swept clean. The single dim bulb in the basement flickered and buzzed.

"Get a grip, Mabel," she told herself.

The stairs creaked under her feet as she descended. Near the bottom, her fear surged again as she peeked around the corner wall. The flickering bulb in front of the clothesline filled with hanging shirts cast erratic, disembodied shapes onto the far stacks of boxes and dusty, disused furniture.

The hairs on the back of her neck began to lift.

Pushing the clothes aside, she went to the wine rack and wrapped her fingers around a cold bottle.

Taking a moment to calm her nerves, she picked up the bottle and—

Ring, ring.

Mabel screamed, dropping the bottle, which shattered on the concrete, spilling the red wine everywhere.

It was the phone upstairs — it must be Kerry!

She raced back upstairs to pick up the receiver in the kitchen. Breathless, she closed the basement door with a satisfying click, not worrying about the mess. "Oh, luv, it's so good to hear from you."

No response.

She frowned. "Kerry? Are you there?"

Nothing.

"Hello!" Mabel said sternly, wondering if this was a prank call. "Who is this?"

A man breathed heavily into the phone.

Mabel huffed. "Isaiah? Jacob? Is that you?"

"Hello, mother."

A shiver ran up her spine, and she nearly dropped the phone.

She gasped, "S-samuel?"

"Yes, mother."

"How dare you call me at home! The police are on to you, you know!"

"You've been a bad mother."

Mabel's grip on the phone tightened. "This is sick. I'm not Angelica!"

He giggled like a girlish child.

"I'm done with this. I am hanging up now, I have police protection and you can't harm me!"

"Then where did your sheriff go?"

Mabel's eyes widened in terror. How could he know this?

With her heart pounding in her chest, she forced herself to lean into the den and peek out the large bay window at the phone booth outside her diner.

A shadowy figure in a dress stared back.

Mabel gasped in horror.

The moon came out from behind the clouds, and she could see the figure, who now looked more like an unnaturally white-faced man in a dress, holding an ax from the woodpile out back.

She dropped the phone horrified, not sure what to do, then stepped forward, stopped, and then just as quickly turned and rushed to the back door to make sure it was locked. Then she ran back to the phone to call Kathy.

Desperately flipping the pages of her notebook back and forth, she found the phone number. Then she peeked to look out the den window toward the payphone and whimpered, seeing the phone dangling from its cord, no one there.

She dialed Kathy, and the phone rang once, twice, three times, then—

"Dispat—"

"Hello! Kathy! Help me!"

Zztt. Click.

"Kathy! I need Dan! Samuel is here, he's here!"

Mabel stared at the receiver. No sounds came from it.

Her voice cracked in fear as she whispered into it, "H-hello?"

No dial tone.

The phone slipped from her hand to bob up and down grotesquely on its stretched cord.

Too exposed in the bright kitchen, she slapped off the light. A lone emergency light within the distant motel burned like the devil's eye.

A step creaked on the front porch.

She snuck another look out the den window. Then caught a flash of a women's dress moving past it toward the front door. Mabel started hyperventilating and backed up.

Thunk!

The front door shook.

She screamed.

Thunk! Thunk!

Wood cracked and splintered as the ax penetrated through the wood. Mabel screamed again and then ran past the den and up the stairs to her bedroom.

She tried the phone by her bed stand — it was dead. The ladder she had used the last time was sitting in her motel office. She hadn't expected to need it again. Trapped upstairs, she ran down the second story hall to go downstairs and out the back door, but—

The broken front door burst open, the ax embedded within it, and Samuel, wearing a wig and grotesque makeup, stepped in, grinning at her.

"I'm home, mother."

Mabel screamed again, backing away as Samuel stepped forward. "Samuel! I'm not your mother. I'm not Angelica!" she pleaded before her terror sent her running back down the hall to her bedroom. Samuel's footfalls raced up the stairs behind. She grabbed her bedroom door's edge to slam it shut when Samuel slammed into her.

She fell back and hit her head against the bed. Then passed out.

* * *

As she regained consciousness, lying on the floor beside her bed, she gasped. Her head ached terribly and her face felt wet. When she patted her cheek, a thick, greasy white and red substance came off on her fingers. It took her a moment to realize it was makeup and not blood.

The bedroom lamps burned bright, and her vision focused on an old woman wiping off makeup in front of the dressing table's mirror. The figure slowly turned around, and it was Samuel smiling cruelly with a mottled white face and red lips.

As he continued wiping the white powder off his face, he said, "I was waiting for you. Normally, I don't let the girls see me like this. But you are different."

"W-what do you want with me?" Mabel edged further back against the bed, but there was nowhere else to go. She looked down the empty hall, willing herself to get up and run, but fear rooted her. Then her hand touched the baseball bat that she had tucked under the bed for protection, and she gripped it tight.

He wiped his eyelids clean with little dabs and then his lips. "You look pretty. Much prettier than me." When he was done, he slowly spun on the stool to casually pick up a knife beside him. "Or my mother."

Mabel acted fast. She pulled out the bat, but he was too quick, crashing into her. He tore the bat from her hands and threw it behind.

A cold knife touched her cheek, and she froze. Samuel was behind her, pressing her down against the side of the bed. His hair mixed with hers, and she could smell his stale breath and feel his heat and excitement.

"Please! Stop!"

He pushed her harder into the side of the bed, and dragged the steel across her cheek, her neck, down her shoulder.

"I'm sorry! Please! I have children!"

"You've hated me since I was born."

"Oh God," Mabel whimpered, unable to move under his weight, feeling the blade dig in. "Samuel!

Samuel!" Mabel pleaded. "I'm not your mother! Please stop this."

He pressed wet lips on her cheek, and in a girlish voice, said, "I always wanted to be like you. I will make you beautiful, mother."

He pushed off her to raise the knife high.

Mabel started to cry, devastated she'd never see her family, friends, loved ones again.

Then the knife fell, cutting deep into the mattress and the bed frame beside her.

She screamed.

His entire body fell onto hers, smothering her, pushing her into the floor.

Then the bulk of him slid past.

Kerry was standing in his place, a baseball bat raised high in her hands. Then she swung it again, slamming it into Samuel's back, and Mabel felt the wallop through him. She pushed herself out from under him as Kerry hit him for a third time. But this time, Samuel did not move. Kerry wound up again, but Mabel cried, "Stop!"

They looked at each other in horror and then back at the man, prone on the floor. Kerry threw the bat away, picked up Mabel and half-dragged her to the door. "Let's get out of here!"

They raced downstairs as a cruiser's lights flashed through the open, shattered front door. Dan rushed in, his gun drawn, as Kerry shouted, "He's upstairs!"

Moving as fast as his large frame could manage, Dan lumbered up the stairs.

Kerry took Mabel into the parking lot, lit only by the red and blue lights. They rested and looked up.

Mabel's bedroom was now in darkness.

The lights had been shut off.

Kerry took off her jacket and wrapped it around Mabel's shoulders. Then started to use her hands to wipe some of the garish makeup off Mabel's face. "What did he do to you?"

Mabel's concern for Dan taking too long overwhelmed her. "Kerry! We've got to protect Dan! He's alone in there!"

"I got this!"

Kerry ran back in, and Mabel stayed out in the cold alone, too frightened to go back in.

Seconds passed. Then minutes. Dan and Kerry did not come out.

Mabel shouted their names, but no one answered.

A horrible feeling that Samuel had overpowered them cowed her. She hesitantly walked up the porch steps, shivering from the shock and cold, ready to flee. Then she took a step inside and peeked up the stairs into the empty shadowed hall above.

She cried out weakly, "Kerry?"

Silence.

Then she whispered, "D-dan?"

A heavy shuffling step scraped along the hall upstairs, coming closer.

Mabel edged backwards, her heart pounding like it would burst from her chest.

A man's profile emerged out of the shadows.

She opened her mouth to scream—

"We got him, Mabel!" Dan shouted. "He's cuffed in the room. And oh boy! Kerry can sure swing a bat!"

Mabel fainted.

CHAPTER 42

Thursday, December 31, 1987

Mabel stood beside John Ford in front of the door leading to the interview room in the Monroe prison. He said, "You don't have to do this."

Mabel looked down at the floor and closed her eyes. "He still hasn't admitted to killing any of the girls, has he?"

"Only his attempt on you. That he was just trying to scare you."

"Well, he certainly did that."

He nodded. "The state's search of his home yielded items from at least four of the missing girls on your list. But it's not enough for a prosecution. Not yet. None of those four are connected to the two bodies we found at Leavenworth."

"Then he won't be charged for any of them?"

John's pained silence said it all.

Mabel sighed. "So, the parents will never know, then?"

"We're hoping he'll tell you."

Mabel looked down at her shoes again. "Because he asked for me."

"Yes."

Mabel shut her eyes to stop herself from reliving the horror of Samuel's knife on her cheek, the heat of his body, the smell of his breath.

"Are you okay? Thanks to you, he'll be in prison for a while."

But it wasn't for life, she thought. She willed herself to stand straighter. "I'm ready," she said, feeling anything but.

John waved to the guard to let them in. "Remember, his shackles are attached to a steel ring in the floor. He can't reach you on your side of the table. The room is wired and the mirror is one-way, so I'll see and hear everything. If you want to leave, just tell me. Everything will be recorded."

The guard opened the door.

Samuel Ketch sat behind a metal table.

Mabel had been warned about his bruised face where Kerry had hit him, but she hadn't anticipated it would remind her of the grotesque makeup he had worn when he had attacked her. A shiver ran down her spine as she stepped into the interview room and found herself alone with him.

The door clanged shut behind her.

"I'm so glad you visited," he said with a smile.

Without knowing what to do or say, her polite nature took over and made her sit, though she scraped the chair back from the table. Her hands were shaking and she struggled to look at him. But when she did, the torment and evil in the hollow pit of his eyes pulled her in, captivating her. And if it weren't for the shackles around his hands and feet, she'd have run. As it was, it took all her strength to remain, and so she focused on John Ford's advice to get through this.

"I'm sorry about your mother," Mabel said at last. She'd learned that Angelica had died the day before Samuel had made his attack on Mabel.

"I'm glad the bitch is dead," Samuel replied, and he visibly relished her shock. "Of course, she was worse when I was a child. But you know that."

Mabel shook her head, and her reply came out in fits and starts. "T-the only thing I remember about that summer is that my dog died. I hadn't remembered anything about you or your mother until I looked through some old photo albums."

A pout passed over his face and he started picking at a broken edge of the metal table with his fingertips, digging in so deep it must have hurt him. "Your father warned her, you know." Samuel glanced up briefly, smiled, and then pressed a nail into the metal. "She was disturbing the other guests. She would yell at me, scream horrible things. The last time we stayed at your motel your father warned her a final time. She was so furious she beat me for that. Then beat me more for crying. It was my fault you see. It was always my fault with her. Did you not know that? Did your father not tell you?"

Mabel shook her head, haunted by their shared past.

His nail cracked and the nail bed bled. But he kept digging into the metal edge, leaving bloody streaks. Mabel glanced to the one-way mirror for guidance, but it reflected only the two of them like they were the only people left in the world. No other sounds filtered in, not even mechanical, and his voice seemed magnified in this room.

"She hated my father, you see. That's why she killed him." Mabel's increasing shock made him smile more. "Doesn't seem so sweet anymore, does she?" He giggled and took on a woman's voice, "Just a little more sugar in your coffee, dear?"

Mabel shivered. It was the same voice he had used when he pressed the knife blade against her skin, and she realized now that Samuel had been imitating his mother when he attacked her. That shook her, and she forced herself to focus on what he was saying.

"Her Alzheimer's exposed her for all to see, or so I had thought. But the docs got it all wrong. They said it was the disease." He shook his head. "But I knew her. It was how she treated me every day of my life. She hated me for who I am. When I was sixteen, she caught me a second time." The blood from his damaged nail smudged into a small red pool. "She beat me harder than ever before until she got scared that she had killed me. I didn't go to school for weeks until I healed."

He kept talking, and Mabel wondered if any of this was true, or whether he was playing a role. She glanced at the mirror again, and he tracked her gaze to their reflection with a frown.

"Did you bring friends, mother?"

She cringed at the word, but then she had a revelation, and she put aside her revulsion as she replied: "Don't focus on them, son."

Samuel blinked several times and then giggled in his chair, trying to curl up in a ball. When that didn't work, he dabbed his finger into the blood on the table and smeared it over his lips. "Do I look pretty, mother?" he asked.

Mabel nodded, suppressing a shudder.

"Do you want to see more?" he asked, now using his thumb to smear blood onto his cheeks. "Do I look beautiful to you now?"

Mabel forced herself not to look away. "Tell me about the girls."

Samuel's thumb froze and then dug into his cheek before he frowned, letting his hand drop to the table and he stayed mute.

"Tell me or I'm going to leave."

He tried to fold his arms across his chest, but the shackles stopped him, frustrating him. "No."

She stood up to leave but was stopped by Samuel's next question.

"Do you know how your dog died?"

That threw Mabel, and she wondered why he would bring that up. "It … it was an animal. Maybe a fox. He was so torn up when I found him. Poor thing."

He smiled while pressing his head to his shoulder like a child keeping a secret.

Her jaw dropped. "It was you!"

"She hated that I wanted to be a girl," he said. Not responding to her accusation that he killed her dog. "Shamed me for it. My father and I would dress in her clothes. We would sit together and have tea. Just the two of us. In makeup and heels." He laughed bitterly and then just as quickly stopped and frowned. "She killed him for that. For finding us. Having our afternoon tea one day wearing her clothes and her wigs. Then she threatened me in the kitchen the day of his funeral and warned me she'd do the same to me if she caught me wearing her finest again."

"I-is that why you hurt the girls?"

Samuel opened his mouth to speak and then glanced at the mirror and shut down.

But Mabel sensed a power over him that she hadn't had before. She said, "If you don't tell me, I'm leaving."

He shrugged, so Mabel turned her back and strode to the door.

"Wait! Please!"

She stopped.

"What do you want to know?"

Mabel closed her eyes. "I want to know about Sandra."

"Stay. Please."

"Only if you tell me about Sandra."

He huffed. She reached for the door handle.

"Fine!"

Steeling herself, Mabel turned and returned to the chair. But this time, she moved it a little closer to him, keeping her back straight and staring deeply into the wells of his brown eyes, no longer afraid of him.

"She was not the first, you know."

"Did you kill her?"

He looked down and picked at the table again.

Mabel moved to leave.

"Fine! So what?"

"Say it," Mabel growled. "Yes or no."

"Yes!"

"Did you bury her in Leavenworth?"

He licked his lips, furtively glancing at the mirror, and then nodded.

"And the other girl, Tracy?"

"I'm not even sure which one she is."

"You saw the newspapers. They had her picture."

"Fine," he replied sullenly. "Yes."

Her voice finally betrayed her. "H-how many in all?

Smirking, he looked down and shrugged. "I don't remember."

"How many? Or I'll leave."

"I don't know. Too many."

"Tell me!" Please, Mabel thought, her gut twisting, feeling like she was back in his grasp, his breath on her neck, his weight upon her, the knife blade against her skin.

After a longer painful pause, he looked into her eyes.

"Twenty-six," he said.

Then the serial killer in him smiled. "If you count my mother too."

CHAPTER 43

Tuesday, January 5, 1988

An expected knock on the front door brought Mabel downstairs. She looked in the hallway mirror to fix her gemstone necklace and then straighten out her dress under her diner apron. Her hair and makeup looked good, but she avoided looking at her eyes in the mirror, too nervous about how this night might turn out.

She took a deep breath and opened the door.

Dan took off his sheriff's hat and said, "Hiya, Mabel." Then gave her a quick once over. "You're all dolled up."

She waved him off. "I just wanted this night to be special."

"Ha! Hopefully not as special as the last one."

Mabel gave Dan a knowing look. Then she stepped onto the porch to slide her arm under his and said, "You mind walking me over to the diner? I just got to pick up some onions. I ran out here."

Dan shrugged. "Sure. Diner's closed early I see. Something special going on?"

"Special?" Her voice rose higher, which she tried to laugh off. "Tuesdays have been so slow with the mine closed so there's no point wasting electricity. The girls don't mind either. Sally and Molly were happy for a break and Kevin's spending time with Lisa before she goes back to school tomorrow."

Dan walked her down the porch steps, and said, "Crazy, seeing all the young ones growing up. Soon, your boys I bet will be going off ta college or something too."

She smiled at first. "Fred? Yes. Hector ... well, we'll see."

Dan chuckled. "A troublemaker like his dad. That's for sure. But none of us went to school, and we turned out alright, I think."

"Some say, Dan. Some say," she replied, but she didn't want to talk about the future tonight. Or the town. Or how her Rotary friends didn't want much of anything to do with her — she didn't care about that so much anymore. So, she said nothing, and Dan didn't either, though he wasn't talkative even at the best of times.

The gravel crunched under their boots.

"Dan?" she asked.

"Yes, ma'am?"

"Don't be mad at me, okay?"

He laughed. "Why? You on another case or something?"

"Something like that."

Dan shook his head ruefully. "I guess we're in for a whole world of trouble then."

She released his arm and took out her diner keys. She paused for a moment, and then opened the door wide as the door chimed. "After you," she said.

Dan nodded, politely, and then stepped in, and froze.

Sitting in the farthest booth away, with candles strewn around the table, was Kennie. He stood up, and though his face betrayed his emotions, he didn't say a word.

Dan backed up and bumped into Mabel. He turned to her and growled, "Mabel! How could you!"

She stood firm. "He wants to talk to you, Dan."

"How dare you bring him here! You know my ma! She'll—"

"She'll not know Dan. This is between us. Between you and Kennie."

"But I can't!"

"You can. You owe it to yourself."

His forehead burst out in a sweat, and he looked down, and she could tell he wanted to flee. So she grasped his sheriff's uniform to stop him from running and shook him gently till he looked at her, his eyes terrified and furious at the same time. "You can leave,

Dan. But what will you be leaving behind?" Then she released him and stepped away, hoping he wouldn't go.

Dan pressed his palms to his stricken face, and for a moment Mabel thought she had lost. That their friendship was done.

But when he finally pulled his hands away, he looked so scared and mad and excited at once. "Gawd Mabel! You make me so emotional!"

She smiled, relieved. Then she adjusted his uniform where she had scrunched the shirt, buttoned up the top button, and brushed stray hairs off his face. "You look good Dan." But he was still stuck in a daze, so she spoke a little louder and sterner this time. "Sheriff Dan Gibson. You are formally invited to dinner at my diner. Will you accept?"

Dan swept back his hair with shaking hands. Then he nodded gruffly, and made his way in. But the pained expression on Kennie's face was now sterner than before, having witnessed Dan's reaction.

When Dan sat down opposite Kennie, neither looked at the other nor said anything, both so timid and uncomfortable. Seeing them struggle so, Mabel poured them glasses of water. "I'm pleased to be able to serve you tonight. I got a beer chilled the way you like it," she said, addressing Dan. "And since Kennie told me his order already and I know what you like to eat, is there anything else you need?"

A red-faced Dan nodded slightly and then turned to face Kennie. He cleared his throat before he said with great emotion, "I'm so sorry for what I done."

Kennie scrunched up his face like he had been slapped and looked down.

Mabel bit her lip, waiting for his response.

After a long moment, a teary-eyed Kennie reached out his hand, and Dan took it, overcome with emotion himself and not hiding his tears of relief either.

Mabel palmed her heart, so pleased.

Then Dan took her hand too, surprising her, and replied to her question, his voice breaking, "It's okay now, Mabel. I've got everything I need right here."

CHAPTER 44

Thursday, January 7, 1988

Mabel looked out at the highway through the diner windows, noting the passing of the police cars accompanied by a forensic van with tinted windows. Throughout the week, these ghastly processions made their way to Pigeon Lake near Leavenworth and then back to the morgue in Seattle. There and back again, and again, until the last of the twenty-five girls had been found.

Detectives had cordoned off the entire area and the site was crawling with forensic investigators, state police, media, and a few hangers-on. She visited once to leave flowers, but a reporter recognized her and started asking questions, and a photo of her was published in the newspapers. John Ford had apologized for that, but the damage was done.

Lavi, visiting from Seattle, was sitting across from her. He had made an excuse to have a piece of her famous pie that Janice, his assistant, raved about, but she suspected it was because of this case and its effect on her. Since her first interview with Samuel at the prison, Mabel had to endure one more session, but at least several agents were alongside her for that one, and Samuel told them what they needed to know. He even bragged about it. Overwhelmed with disgust and horror, she made an excuse to leave and ended up in a washroom stall, sobbing uncontrollably.

Apparently, her diner was even involved in Samuel's killing ritual. After he had murdered a woman, dressed her up, and buried her, he would wash off in the lake, change his clothes, and stop at her diner for a coffee.

Try as she might, Mabel couldn't remember him. His visits were months apart, and he likely kept to himself. On the rare occasions that she'd been his server, she had probably smiled at him and, like with most obvious loners, gave him space to feel at home. Many people passed through this town, some chatty, some not, but together a strange mix of tourists, nature lovers, miners, forestry workers, truckers, bikers, and eccentrics. Not once had she suspected her customers to be murderers too. She didn't know what to think about that. It seemed a betrayal of all that she held dear, that her gift for reading people had not stopped this man until too late.

After the police procession had passed, Lavi put down his fork and said kindly, "Their families will have peace now."

Mabel nodded and went back to toying with the food on her plate.

Lavi waited and then filled in the silence. "This pie is wonderful. Even with all Janice's praise, she didn't do it justice."

Mabel forced a thin smile, too depressed to respond to his compliment.

Then he leaned in to get her attention. "You did good. You should be proud of yourself. I have many more cases in the wings if you want to keep yourself occupied."

"I'm not ready for that."

"You're the best investigator I've got. And, my word Mabel, there are law professors like I said writing chapters of textbooks on our work. Student lawyers and legal experts will learn about what we've done."

Mabel looked at her hands — a working girl's hands. Tough and lean. "I'm tired, Lavi. This case … it … took a lot out of me."

"How could it not? A serial killer was in your home, threatening you."

Mabel nodded, but it wasn't quite that. While Samuel no longer terrified her in person, he still haunted her dreams. She told him, "Kerry was amazing, of course. I was so impressed by her standing up for me. Confronting Samuel. Apparently, her FBI mentor gave her the nickname Babe Ruth." Lavi looked confused, so she explained. "After a famous baseball player, I guess."

Lavi shrugged, never being much into sports either. "Well, if she's truly looking for a career in the FBI and she's half as good as you, she'll be a star."

Mabel nodded, feeling proud of her niece who was becoming more like a daughter every day.

The door chimed.

Mabel slowly turned to look—

And froze.

Samuel Ketch walked in, wearing a baseball cap, turtleneck, and dark clothes, and he stared at her to reveal his toothy, evil grin—

"Mabel!"

Mabel blinked — and the face of Samuel morphed into another man. A newcomer to the diner, who took a seat at the counter.

Lavi touched her arm and repeated gently, "Mabel."

She looked over at Lavi, embarrassed. More and more she had been seeing evil walk through her door. And it made her wonder about her sanity. She breathed in and out to calm herself and then smiled as best she could to hide her discomfort.

"For a second, you seemed to drift off."

She leaned over her plate, uncomfortable, but eventually looked him in the eyes. "I can't help thinking about what Samuel said. About how his mother treated him." She paused, feeling her gut twisting. "Now, I don't know whether everything he said was real or not. But he did tell us where he had buried those girls. And

I met his mother, and she scared me. And I could only imagine how terrible it must have been to have been raised by her and how she treated him, especially with what he was struggling with."

"Killing those girls wasn't his mother's fault."

"I know," Mabel said, feeling the guilt all mothers feel. "It just makes me think of myself as a mother. How I have treated my sons, and how I could do better. You know my work for you here has put my sons in harm's way, and no matter what good came out of it—"

"Lots."

She acknowledged that with a nod, but that wasn't her point. "It just makes me want to be a better mom, is all. I feel guilty for how I'm raising them and now with Bill gone again, though he's trying to get better, I just wonder what home life I'm giving them. I'm not Angelica, by any means, but it's just..." she paused and sighed.

"You need to be careful about what you take away from a killer like Samuel. He wants you to think he is a victim. But he's a manipulator who preys on the insecurities of others. It's pretty clear how much being a mother means to you and he was using that."

"Maybe so."

"Look. I think of my mom. She's going through dementia and it pains me so to see her like that. She was always so loving, caring and kind but now, she forgets me..." Lavi winced and paused. "And yes, I remember those times when she wasn't the perfect mother, but I wasn't the perfect son either. Everyone makes mistakes. It is what you learn from those mistakes that makes all the difference."

He paused to take a sip of coffee. "People like Samuel and Angelica, yes, they had a horrible relationship, but Samuel's psychosis goes back before the day he was born. Angelica's too. What horrible things they did was entirely due to their inherent diseased psychoses, not due to any mother-son dynamic or with his emerging gender-identity. We all make mistakes Mabel. You are as human as anyone else." He paused, but she didn't know how to respond, so he went on. "Look. I say you're my best investigator not because you're perfect, but because you don't stop. And with your boys, you will never stop being the best mother you can be to them. And yes, you will screw up and make mistakes like any parent, but it's how you deal with it afterwards. That's just what being a parent is — at least that's what my mom tells me and she's a pretty amazing mom. And you remind me of her."

Mabel stared off in the direction of the distant hills of Leavenworth. "I'm just ... It's just that those mothers won't have a chance to fix their mistakes." Her voice sounded scarred. "Their parenting was cut short the moment that monster took their daughters away. Whatever they had done as a parent up to that moment will be what they judge themselves on as a mother, good or bad. And my heart goes out to them for that."

Lavi touched Mabel's hand. "Are you okay?"

Mabel used a napkin to stem her tears and Lavi stayed silent, giving her time.

She huffed, embarrassed for her emotions. "I'm sorry, Lavi."

"That's okay," he said. "It's that heart of yours that makes you so special too."

She smiled, tearing up again, but in a good way. She squeezed his hand to show how much she appreciated what he said. He blushed and said, "Well in other news, Paul Hammetts is free. He wants to thank you in person if he could."

Mabel pulled her hand away and gave Lavi a shocked look. "If he wants to thank me, tell him never to harm a child again."

"I thought you would say that."

Mabel couldn't stay mad at Lavi for long. She noticed his coffee cup was empty so she picked up the coffee urn on the table and filled his cup before she filled her own. He thanked her as he added in cream and sugar.

"I don't know, Lavi. Working with you this past year I've started to see more and more of the bad side of people. Take Samuel. He says I served him coffee and made him feel at home. How could I not see him for what he was? How did I not know that he murdered girls?" She examined the faces of her customers around her. "What horrible secrets are hidden within those that visit my diner? What am I missing here?"

"You've seen things that have opened your eyes is all. You'll be a better investigator for it."

Mabel shook her head. "It makes me feel … jaded somehow. That this little feeling of home I've always wanted to provide here is not enough to make this world a better place." She rubbed her arms and shivered. "I am an optimist, and I don't want to see people as evil. That's not me. It doesn't sustain me."

"It's wisdom."

"Is it?" Mabel asked, not believing it. "I don't feel wiser. In fact, I feel like my eyes have been opened to a world I suspected but never acknowledged. I thought I could build a safe haven here in Blue River for my family, but I was wrong."

"My God, Mabel," Lavi said, briefly throwing his hands in the air. "Think of what you've done. You caught the real killers of Karen Thompson, you ended Larson's massive drug operation and freed six abducted girls, and you tracked down a serial killer! That's incredible. You're being written into textbooks for having been part of the second DNA case in the country, let alone these last two! And from what I hear from John Ford, he's asked you to give an informal talk to his FBI recruits later this summer. He tells me your interview with Samuel was like watching a master class. Be kind to yourself, Mabel. You deserve it."

Mabel sipped her coffee to give herself time to think of a response. But she had nothing to tell him, so she noted idly, "I make a good cup of coffee." Then looked at Lavi's empty plate. "Are you still hungry, dear? You've got a long drive back and I worry about you."

Lavi gave her a sly look. "No, I'm good. My mom says hi to you by the way. She adores you, you know."

"She's wonderful."

Lavi wiped his mouth with his napkin and then finished the last of his coffee. "You do have the best coffee that's true." He collected his things and stood up along with her. "You avoided my question about working with me again, but just think about it, alright? I'll call soon."

Mabel touched his arm and then guided him out. Then she waited outside in the cold to wave to him one last time as his car pulled out onto the highway. Folding her arms to ward off the chill, she looked over the road, the forest, the mountain, and the sky, and it was beautiful.

CHAPTER 45

Sunday, January 10, 1988

Mabel finished a joke to a trucker eating his steak and eggs. The trucker's eyes widened, and he laughed, spitting out some of his meal. "That's a good one, Mabel!" he said, slapping the counter.

She topped up his coffee with a smile, then lightly tapped his shoulder as she moved past to serve Mike Wiggley, a local eccentric, rumored to be sitting on a pile of money, who had just sat down in his usual booth. A friend and a regular, he often regaled her on how he was going to transform Blue River into the next skiing mecca. She didn't quite buy into his vision of rich people paying so much to ski here. But that was okay. He told good tales.

Kevin shouted from the kitchen. "Mabel! Phone call. It's that lawyer friend of yours — Lavi."

Mabel paused, gazing around her place, which was busier than normal. And it was only going to get busier again with the next phase of mine construction about to begin. Her youngest, Fred, was sitting at the diner counter, doing homework, while Hector was off with friends, Kerry was back at college and her Bill was somewhere getting sober. It wasn't an easy life, but it was hers.

She acknowledged Kevin with a wink and a smile. "Tell Lavi I'm busy."

Then she filled Mike's cup to the brim and asked, "You got another story for me, luv?"

The End of Book 3

MORE BOOKS BY THE AUTHOR

Mabel Davison Historical Mystery Series
Heart of a Runaway Girl
Missed Me
Haunting Pasts

Jack Winters Historical Adventure Series
Winter Sands (Publishing 2024)

ABOUT THE AUTHOR

Trevor Wiltzen is passionate about crafting stories featuring relatable characters facing extraordinary circumstances. He resides in Edmonton, Alberta, a small big-city on the prairies. Alongside writing, he enjoys spending quality time with his wife, two beautiful boys, and their friendly dogs. Wiltzen is the creative mind behind the Mabel Davison historical mystery series and is presently working on developing two new intersecting mystery and adventure series.

Readers can keep up with his latest work and receive free content by subscribing to his e-newsletter on his website, www.trevorwiltzen.com/books. Additionally, fans can follow him on Amazon, Goodreads, and Bookbub to stay updated on his latest releases.

Made in the USA
Las Vegas, NV
28 October 2024

10602169R00184